THE INSPIRING STORY OF LAILA

HARLEEN MAKAR

Copyright © Harleen Makar 2022
All Rights Reserved.

ISBN 979-8-88783-341-5

This book has been published with all efforts taken to make the material error-free after the consent of the author. However, the author and the publisher do not assume and hereby disclaim any liability to any party for any loss, damage, or disruption caused by errors or omissions, whether such errors or omissions result from negligence, accident, or any other cause.

While every effort has been made to avoid any mistake or omission, this publication is being sold on the condition and understanding that neither the author nor the publishers or printers would be liable in any manner to any person by reason of any mistake or omission in this publication or for any action taken or omitted to be taken or advice rendered or accepted on the basis of this work. For any defect in printing or binding the publishers will be liable only to replace the defective copy by another copy of this work then available.

Contents

Preface 5
Acknowledgements. 7

1. The Phone Call 9
2. From Dehradun to Delhi. 15
3. Migration: A Mixed Blessing 21
4. Bittersweet Experiences. 26
5. The Roof Lays the Foundation 31
6. A Hair-Raising Beginning to The New Year. 35
7. The Wedding Invitation. 40
8. An Enjoyable Trip. 45
9. Laila on a Sticky Wicket. 51
10. Nina Falls and Rises Thereafter 56
11. A Tale of Accomplishments. 61
12. Emotional Strings 65
13. Tough and Trying Times 69
14. Buddy's Absence 73
15. Mrs Samson's Health Issues. 78
16. A New Beginning for Laila 84
17. That Scary Month. 88
18. Here Comes Turmoil 92
19. The Mishmash of Emotions 97
20. Mixed Bag 101
21. Not Again! 105
22. The Ever-Gracious Mrs Samson. 110

23. The Growth Phase 113
24. The New Couple 119
25. Renovation? 124
26. Unanticipated 129
27. The Race Against Time 132
28. Out of Sorts 134
29. Care and Concern 139
30. Nina's Wedding 146
31. The Aftereffects 152
32. The Short-lived Calm 157
33. Laila—The Star 162
34. Inquisitive Parents 166
35. Nina Moves Abroad 170
36. Trouble in Paradise 174
37. On Pins and Needles 181
38. Recovery and Then a Huge Loss 185
39. Back to the Roots 189

Preface

Dear Reader,

This is the story of a girl named Laila. Tracing four decades of her life, it highlights the inspirational and insightful aspects of her journey.

I've been writing poetry around the theme of gratitude and relationships for a long time and firmly believe that, as individuals, our integral values and credibility matter the most. One day, I felt compelled to pen down a few random sentences on the existence of unmatched selflessness and commitment in this world where we belong. In those moments, my thoughts were centred around pushing beyond limits to fulfil responsibilities. Once those few sentences turned into a couple of pages, the story of Laila took shape. And months later, this little book appeared on the white sheets, unannounced.

I thoroughly enjoyed writing this book, and I hope you feel the same excitement as you read it. I consider myself a poet first, and that is why every chapter culminates with an introspective poetic piece which resonates with the theme.

Every new book is a tribute
To those who've read the earlier ones;
For an author, readership is like
A starry shower from the heavens.

Thank you and enjoy reading!
Harleen Makar

Acknowledgements

I'm extremely grateful to my loving parents. Had it not been for their persuasion to diversify my writing, this book would not have seen the light of day. Supporting my ideas and offering valuable insights, they made the process incredibly exciting for me.

The Phone Call

The warm fragrance of freshly-baked muffins and perfectly brewed coffee was spreading from the kitchen to the veranda, and Mrs Samson, out of sheer impatience, started moving towards the coffee table. When young, she was anything but slow! However, now, due to weak bones, she was dependent on a walker that had cut down her pace. She saw Laila, her help, exit the kitchen with a loaded tray in her hands. Being a lover of baked delicacies, she couldn't resist moving fast and lost her balance, unfortunately. Seeing the frail lady land on the floor with the walker's rails hitting her right on her ribs, Laila screamed, "Madam!"

As fast as she could, she put the tray on the table in the lobby and ran towards Mrs Samson, and helped her turn over. Blood was oozing from her right eyebrow and elbow and she wasn't able to move her shoulder. Laila rushed towards the gate and opened it in haste. She shouted, "Raju, come fast. Madam has had a fall!"

Raju, the driver, who was basking in the sun, rushed inside. Both of them somehow managed to lift Mrs Samson up and helped her lie on the couch. A doctor arrived in the next few minutes, bandaged her wounds, and prescribed medicines.

Initially, Mrs Samson was in pain. However, after a few hours, she felt better. Subsequently true to her jovial nature, she softly asked Laila for the muffins that had started off the terrible ordeal that day! A very accustomed Laila smiled and got them for her.

"Where is the sauce?" asked Mrs Samson. Laila quickly reached out to the bottle on the dining table, flipped open the lid, and gave it to her. Generously loading the muffins with chocolate sauce, Mrs Samson ate a couple of them and later retired to bed.

The next morning, all three of them visited a hospital to get an x-ray done as advised by the doctor. While they were returning home, Laila got a call from Nina, her half-sister, who lived with her mother in a small village in Chakrata, Dehradun. Nina, all of twelve years, was crying inconsolably. She could barely speak. However, in a quivering voice, she managed to tell Laila about the untimely demise of their mother. The news left Laila shocked and numb, but she soon pulled herself together, as she realized that Nina would now be all alone. Her father, Laila's stepfather, had unfortunately passed away five years ago in a road accident.

By the time the sun went down, Laila packed a few clothes in a small red-coloured travel bag and got ready to leave for her village. While Raju dropped her off at the railway station, he continued to console her, as deep pain and grief rolled down her cheeks in the form of tears. She boarded the train and told Raju, "Take care of Madam." It was a rare occurrence that they had to leave Mrs Samson under the care of neighbours while both of them were away.

Raju then drove for another fifty kilometres to bring his wife, Sarita, who generally filled-in for Laila whenever needed. It was half-past midnight when Raju and Sarita reached home. Mrs Samson slept till late the next morning, as she had a terribly anxious night. When she woke up, Sarita served her lentil soup and whole-wheat tomato sandwiches. The lady took the first bite and said, "Sarita, you know I don't like cottage cheese in my sandwiches!"

"I know Madam, but the doctor has added it to your diet chart. You need more calcium and proteins."

"Laila also does the same!" exclaimed Mrs Samson.

By late afternoon, Laila called to inform Mrs Samson that she had reached her village. Both Mrs Samson and Laila broke down while they were talking on the phone. When Mrs Samson enquired about Nina, Laila replied, "The poor child had to be admitted to a nearby hospital by my mother's friends before I arrived, as she was running a high fever and had turned non-responsive."

Mrs Samson sighed and exclaimed, "Oh Lord, show mercy!" However, the very next moment, she was relieved upon knowing that with medical intervention, Nina had regained consciousness and was now resting in the warm embrace of Laila.

Sarita, who stood beside Mrs Samson, gently placed her baby on the old lady's lap and took the receiver from her, as she sensed Mrs Samson's growing uneasiness. She talked to Laila for a while and later got busy with work.

A little less than a year ago, Sarita and Raju had been blessed with a baby boy, whom they had lovingly named Harsh. Harsh brought back Mrs Samson's smile while he playfully lay on her lap and she fondly sang him a lullaby.

Back in the hills, it was a chilly morning, and there had been a light drizzle, barely enough to wet the ground.

The curtain of haze obliterated the picturesque view of the mountains. Laila hadn't slept the whole night. She mourned her loss, remembering her mother and reliving old memories of the times when she had missed home after first moving to Delhi for work. On the other hand, she sank deep into thoughts about Nina's future – her grief, her tender age, and everything that was to come.

Laila said to herself, "Although I've been supporting my family financially for the last three years, at this juncture I feel so weak. I don't know if I'll be able to stand the mounting pressure of responsibilities." The twenty-one-year-old felt intimidated. Under distress, tears rolled down her pale cheeks once again. The glow on her sharp-featured face was dampened by tears and her swollen eyelids spoke of pain. However, she closed her eyes, folded her hands, and started praying.

In the meantime, Nina woke up and called for her. "Good morning. I'll just get your glass of milk, Nina," Laila responded. The child had the habit of waking up early, as she was enrolled in a school which was about a kilometre away from her village. This was also one of Laila's major concerns, as it was mid-term, and shifting Nina out would set her studies back by one full year. If she stayed back with Nina, she would lose her job which would mean no income at all.

With such thoughts upsetting her frame of mind, she got up from the chair and went towards the kitchen. They didn't have a refrigerator at home. The milk used to be delivered in the morning by the milkman. Nina liked her milk warm, not hot. Laila heated the milk, but before she could reach Nina, the sky started to roar. There was lightning and the clouds seemed to be angry. Loud thunders were heard. Their village was in the foothills, thus almost everyone was acclimatised to dense clouds and heavy rainfall. However, their current predicament had shaken the girls to the core making them more vulnerable.

The scared child screamed, ran towards her sister, and clung to her tightly. That very moment, Laila said to herself, "I can't go to Delhi leaving Nina behind in the care of any of our relatives even if it's just for a few months."

The next few days kept both of them busy with rituals and prayers for their departed mother's soul. Once Laila had some free time, she called Mrs Samson who had been waiting to hear from her. A hesitant and unsure Laila didn't know if Mrs Samson would agree to Nina living with them in Delhi. She was in a situation where she needed her job now more than ever, which itself was at stake.

While she mustered the courage to speak, wishing for things to go smoothly, she heard the most reassuring words from Mrs Samson. "When are you and Nina coming to Delhi? I am worried about both of you, and have you got her transfer certificate from school?"

An emotional talk ensued between the two of them. Whatever Laila knew of her, Mrs Samson was a lady of few words. At that moment, Laila realised that every minute over the past two years which she had spent working at Mrs Samson's house had actually gone into building the foundation for a subtle and beautiful bond. Losing her mother had surely destabilized her, but now she was able to see Mrs Samson as her Godmother and she felt that the old lady had her back.

Nina, who was in the adjacent room, heard a part of the conversation. Unaware of the purpose of that conversation, and unsettled by the thought that her sister was talking to 'Madam' in Delhi, she ran towards the trunk on which Laila's red bag lay. Out of insecurity and fear of being left alone, she hid it under her bed.

Laila, who on the other hand, was much relieved and eager to break the news to Nina, looked around for her but the little one was nowhere to be seen. Despite calling her name repeatedly, Nina didn't show up. Laila got anxious and ran outside to look for her. Running helter-skelter, looking for the little girl and calling out her name repeatedly, she finally spotted the child beside a tree. Nina was crying and her face was all red. On coaxing her to open up, Nina spoke of her insecurities. Laila hugged her and wiped her tears. Excitedly, she told the little girl about the phone call and the new journey on which they were to embark.

**Away from home, working tirelessly, to make ends meet,
Millions miss out on synchronizing with their loved ones'
heartbeats.**

From Dehradun to Delhi

A week later, sitting on a bench with her sister, Nina playfully nibbled on a yellow and pink cotton candy roll. Laila, meanwhile, seated alongside two overstuffed bags, waited for the train to arrive at the platform. She fondly ran her fingers over the embroidery on her red bag as if to feel her mother's touch. Her mother had hand-embroidered Laila's initials on the bag and had given it to her when she had first left for Delhi. It surely was a precious possession.

"I had carried along my dreams and aspirations in this bag when I moved to the city for work. However, from this day onward, Nina's welfare will always be my first priority," Laila thought to herself as if to reassure her mother.

Amidst the ongoing announcements at the railway station, Nina asked, "Are there any kids at Mrs Samson's house? I am going to miss my friends! Who will play with me?"

Just when Laila was about to respond, the train arrived. She told the child, "Get up quickly and hold my hand till we board the train safely."

It was the first time that Nina was going to travel, as she had not stepped out of the village in her twelve years. When her father was alive, he would keep going back and forth between the village and the town where he worked. Her mother was a daily-wager at an apple orchard near the village.

As soon as they got to their berth, an excited Nina asked, "Can I take the upper one? I want to, please?" Laila helped her get up there while giving her strict safety instructions. The wheels of the train started to roll and so did those of their destiny, in a new direction.

It was a ten-hour journey, and Nina was just not ready to take her mid-day nap. She wanted to capture and save each and every scene in her eyes. The green landscapes, the sight of clouds playing with the mountains, the waterfalls, the herds of cattle grazing far away – such scenes were marking the transition to the next phase. Somehow, the train's speed symbolized the dynamism of time.

After a few hours, Nina insisted on coming to the lower berth from where she could enjoy the view through the window. A doting Laila, wanting to give her all the happiness that she could, allowed her to do so. She wanted to help the child tide over the grief of losing her mother.

Later, the train stopped at a station midway. It was snack time, and Laila told Nina, "Let's get down to buy some tea and cookies."

Nina was quick enough to say, "Not cookies but chocolates!" While they waited at the tea stall for their order, Laila spotted Ronit, her childhood friend, whom she hadn't met in the last three years. He was travelling in another coach on the same train and was supposed to take the next train from Delhi.

Ron, as he preferred to be addressed by everyone in the village, excitedly told Laila, "I got selected in the Army and am going to join the forces as a soldier."

A visibly ecstatic Laila congratulated and praised him. Suddenly the train's siren went off and they had to rush back. After a while, Ron came to meet her in their compartment. He was an enthusiastic young boy who was excitedly embarking on a journey to realize his cherished dream. They chatted for quite a while catching up on each other's lives.

Later, Ron returned to his seat. Both the girls then had dinner and slept. Just past midnight, they reached Delhi. As they were deboarding, Laila spotted Raju. Mrs Samson had made sure that Raju was there before time to bring the girls home safely. The lady's kind-heartedness was ever evident in her actions.

Cities undeniably have a liveliness of their own, vastly different from the calmness offered by the hills. There is a general hustle and bustle and the roads are jam-packed with vehicles. Attractively lit tall buildings line the horizon beautifully at night. The contrast is such that it stuns and attracts any newcomer, especially, someone from the peaceful and sparsely populated foothills. Nina was excited to see the busy lanes and beautifully lit highways. She kept asking questions about the newness she saw.

It was pitch dark when they arrived and Mrs Samson was sleeping. Sarita had put her baby to sleep and had added another cot in Laila's room for little Nina. She had also prepared some food for them, as she knew that the girls would be hungry by the time they reached home.

Mrs Samson also had two Labradors, Brown and Buddy. They had sensed that someone new was coming home and due to restlessness, they were also awake. As soon as the car arrived, they ran towards the gate to meet Laila. The child was very excited to see them. Back there in the village, she loved playing with cats, rabbits, and goats and had made friends with a few canines too. Wagging their tails, trying to climb up the girls, they showered a lot of affection on Laila and Nina.

At about 7:00 a.m., when Mrs Samson was served bed-tea, she exclaimed, "Laila, my child, what a tough time you've been through. I am so relieved to see that you're back." Holding her hand tightly, she continued, "You must be tired. Did you get to sleep for some time?"

A visibly touched Laila responded, "Yes Madam, I am fine. I am glad to see that your wounds have healed completely."

A few hours later, she woke Nina up and brought her down from the room on the second floor. It was going to be Nina's first interaction with Mrs Samson!

Mrs Samson's house was large. The ground floor was where Mrs Samson spent most of her time. The first floor had fully furnished rooms for guests and family. The second floor had one room, a kitchen, and a bathroom. That was where Laila used to rest at night.

Such was the love and liveliness hidden inside Mrs Samson's heart that by the evening, Nina was seen braiding and decorating her long, grey hair with multicoloured clips. Meanwhile, Sarita and baby Harsh left for their home, and it was time for Laila to take Brown and Buddy for their walk. Nina asked her, "Can I accompany you? I don't want to stay alone."

Laila replied, "You aren't alone Nina. Mrs Samson is here with you. I will be back soon." The child agreed, but reluctantly.

Nina was a very inquisitive and observant child. She began her queries about the people she saw in the tastefully arranged frames in Mrs Samson's room. The old lady responded in detail. She told Nina that she was a mother to two sons who were settled abroad with their families and the three little kids in the pictures were her grandchildren. She said, "Initially, my sons had moved abroad for higher studies, but eventually they settled miles and miles away from their homeland!"

Twenty minutes later, Laila returned. Leaning against the wall, she listened to Mrs Samson as the lady poured her heart out. Mrs Samson continued, "When my sons were studying in college and during the initial years of their career, they came home every other year for vacations. It used to be the most joyous time of the year. Their kids would play, eat and go with me to the park. This was the only time of the year when the rooms on the first floor had occupants."

Soon, Nina's interest shifted to the colourful dream-catcher hanging in the room. Mrs Samson acknowledged Laila's presence and went on, "During the rest of the year, the rooms were empty yet ready in anticipation. My husband and I vacillated between excitement and gloom accordingly."

Once her husband passed away, Mrs Samson became more lonely. To tide over the phase of grief, initially, she spent some time abroad with both her sons and their families. But, the independent, bold lady in her knew that she wanted to return to her country and live life on her own terms. While talking about the tough phase, she teared up.

In an attempt to shift focus and change the mood, Laila asked, "Madam, what should I make for dinner?"

"I feel like having baked beans today," Mrs Samson said.

That evening was Nina's first time at a dining table. Mrs Samson took time to teach her some graceful etiquette as the child relished continental food which was very new to her, but regular fare at Mrs Samson's house.

Changes are just destiny's ways to put our strength to test;
We must learn to neither label them as challenges nor detest.

03

Migration: A Mixed Blessing

A couple of years passed by. One day, when Laila was seated in the audience at the annual function at Nina's school, she got a call from Ron. She was pleasantly surprised to hear from him after a considerable gap. They had last interacted during their train journey.

Ron had a layover in Delhi before proceeding to his village on his annual leave. Later that evening, with Mrs Samson's permission, Laila met Ron at a nearby cafe. Away from her duties, it was a nice break for Laila. They shared fond memories, participated in light-hearted banter, and reminisced about their childhood as Nina sipped her chocolate milkshake totally absorbed, and in complete awe of her surroundings. Prior to this day, Nina had never visited a fancy cafe although Laila used to take her out to budget eateries once in a while.

On returning home, the girls saw Mrs Samson beaming with joy. She couldn't contain her excitement, and as soon as they entered the living room, she said, "Laila, Eric called to say that he will be visiting India with his family in a fortnight. I am so happy!" Eric was Mrs Samson's elder son.

All her ailments seemed to have disappeared as she started briefing Laila about the arrangements that were to be done. The next ten days were very hectic for Laila. From washing the curtains, cleaning the upholstery, and checking the functionality of electronics to tidying up the cabinets and cupboards, she did everything. She did all this while taking care of Mrs Samson's daily requirements. She had the amazing quality of preserving her smile while carrying on with her chores.

A day before Eric and his family were to leave for India, he called Mrs Samson and informed her that due to work commitments his wife and younger grandson would not be able to come. Suddenly, the old lady's enthusiasm vanished and she exclaimed, "This is not done! I've been waiting for so long for all of you to come home."

It was tough for Mrs Samson to overcome this brief yet intense period of waning excitement. However, she found solace at the thought of Eric's and Jeffrey's forthcoming visit. Jeffrey was Eric's elder son.

A few days later, on a bright morning, Laila suddenly heard Nina crying. She ran from the kitchen towards the dining area where Nina was having breakfast. "What happened? Did you hurt yourself while eating?" she asked Nina.

While Laila attended to Nina, Jeffry got up from his chair and ran upstairs. He was the same age as Nina. Nina shook her head and said, "Jeffry told me that I should go back to my village because this is his granny's house. I never said, it was mine! Why can't we go back? Why did Mom leave me alone?" she asked sobbing.

Mrs Samson got worried. In the past two years, never had she seen this side of Nina. She was saddened to the core. Laila calmed Nina down and urged her to finish breakfast.

With every passing day since her arrival in Delhi, Nina got more accustomed to city life. She played with her friends in the park till late evening which was never the case in the village. There were numerous comforts that made life easier. From the mere availability of ice, cold water, a television set for entertainment, a wide variety of food items, to the ready availability of almost everything, the adaptation to city life was a major and pleasurable change for the child. However, Jeffrey's comment struck her really hard. All of a sudden, she wanted to return to the village.

Mrs Samson, at an opportune time, talked about the issue with her son and told him to pay attention to Jeffry's bullying behaviour. She said to him, "This is the tender age at which children develop virtues and in turn, an empathetic nature if guided in the right way. You should pay more attention to your child's attitude during these formative years." She felt embarrassed, and her grandmotherly feelings peaked at this juncture.

Deep inside, Mrs Samson felt that had her grandchildren been living with her, she could have contributed much more to their upbringing. She and Mr Samson had always been very appreciative of the concept of joint families, as they had been brought up like that. The desertion caused by the distance hit them hard after their children settled abroad. Initially, they found it very tough to adjust to their sons not being there for them. Later, they made peace with reality, as they knew that their loneliness could never be filled-in for. Evidently, they were not restrictive as parents, and the feelings that sat in the depths of their hearts always remained unshared.

That pep talk, however, didn't go down very well with Mrs Samson's son. He had never been appreciative of the fact that at various points in time, family members of the house-helps stayed at the servants' quarters of the house. He said, "Mom, this issue wouldn't have cropped up if Nina wasn't living here. Why don't you employ professional caretakers who have no strings attached?"

This infuriated the old lady. "Why not! Just like your policy of settling abroad with no strings attached!" she said, tearing up. She had never thought that she would say this to her son one day.

Laila heard everything. She felt all the more embarrassed as she held herself responsible for this escalation. There was a lull and all three of them had dinner in their respective rooms. Laila had a sleepless night. Mrs Samson had supported her all these years, and she felt helpless on seeing the lady's laughter turn into tears.

The next day, things calmed down a bit and Laila cooked Jeffry's favourite pasta. She baked some muffins for the mother-son duo in an attempt to bring back their smiles. She succeeded to a great extent. She advised Nina not to get into any further spats with Jeffry and instead, spend more time studying or playing in their room on the second floor.

Laila figured that it wasn't a case of Mrs Samson's son not being caring enough. Rather, it was a mismatch of thoughts and a generation gap. Days passed by peacefully. Every day, Mrs Samson would give Jeffrey some surprise – a toy, a t-shirt, some chocolates, a game, etc. Finally, Eric and Jeffrey left after their vacation was over. Raju dropped them off at the airport as Mrs Samson sat in the car, waving and blowing kisses to them. Her tears told a deeper story. After all, distances bother the elders more than the younger lot.

> Stop for a while and think if you can – about your words,
> Your deeds, your decisions, the unsaid, and all that goes
> unheard.

04

Bittersweet Experiences

On a lazy afternoon, as the sun outside painted the sky in various shades of orange and grey, Nina screamed, "DG!" and started giggling. By then, Nina had started fondly addressing Mrs Samson as "DG," the acronym for Dear Granny. Both of them were sitting under the shade of an umbrella and DG was playfully tickling little Nina as the duo played a round of Scrabble.

Laila was busy in the kitchen, preparing delicious snacks for a small party in the evening. Nina won that round of Scrabble, and as agreed upon beforehand, she got to wear a pretty green beaded necklace from Mrs Samson's jewellery collection for the party.

It was little Harsh's birthday and Mrs Samson had planned a celebration. Later that evening, Raju brought Sarita and Harsh to Mrs Samson's house. Three of Nina's friends, who lived in the neighbourhood, were also invited to the party. Nina got all dressed up. Adjusting the gorgeous piece on her neckline, she said to Mrs Samson, "Thanks DG, your necklace makes me feel like a princess!" The old lady was very happy to hear this.

The kids played games and were extremely excited to cuddle baby Harsh, so much so that they weren't ready to put him down on the floor. They just wanted to hold him in their slender arms. Mrs Samson was gracious enough to play Dumb Charades with everyone and she even won a round. It was a great celebration and everyone had fun.

The next morning, Mrs Samson asked them if they wanted to go for a picnic. Although they were ready, they were concerned about her health. Considering her age, they thought that such an outing might be tiring for her. But she had always been a child at heart!

On her insistence, they set off for Damdama Lake which was about sixty kilometres away from Delhi. A calm place near the Aravalli Hills, it had camel rides, food stalls, and a multitude of swings for kids. A famous picnic spot, it was known for its biodiversity.

It was quite sunny when they reached the lake. The old lady spotted a stall that had colourful hats on display. She bought hats for each member in their favourite colours. Baby Harsh's hat kept falling off due to his tiny head. However, Nina tirelessly set it right every time. Then, they all sat down and ordered some pasta and pizzas.

Next, it was time for fun rides for the kids. They went on the slides, the swings, and the merry-go-round but they enjoyed the paddle boats the most. After spending about three hours there, they started off for home. Both Nina and Harsh were exhausted and slept on the way back. All of a sudden, Mrs Samson got emotional and a tear trickled down her cheek onto Laila's hand. Laila noticed it and asked, "What happened, Madam, are you alright?"

To this, the old lady replied, "Nothing, just old memories!"

She then went on to talk about picnics that she and her husband used to plan for the kids when they were little. Very often, they explored the outskirts of the city and had lots of fun playing and eating outside in green, open spaces. It was only when her kids grew up to be teenagers that they started enjoying themselves more with their friends than their parents. Since then, she had not enjoyed a picnic like this one.

"Our last picnic together was quite eventful. It was a chilly morning, and the boys had their mid-session break. Mr Samson had a day off from work, so we decided to take the kids out. We were unaware that the kids had made plans for a football match with their neighbourhood gang." Mrs Samson paused to remove her glasses and wipe off the tears. She continued, "I still remember, I prepared snacks and cookies and packed juice in travel safe bottles in a jiffy before the kids had woken up. We had planned to surprise them. We were eager and thought it would make them super excited. However, much to our disappointment, the boys refused straight away!"

"I can't even imagine the disappointment you must have felt," Laila said.

Mrs Samson agreed with her saying, "Yes! I felt like crying. I had been up early, preparing all their favourite food items. That day, for the first time, we got a taste of our children being teenagers."

Sarita expressed her own apprehension saying, "I don't know what I'll do when Harsh enters his teens. This seems emotionally draining!"

Mrs Samson nodded and continued with her story and revealed that a few hours later, after much deliberation, they did reach the picnic spot, but they were not alone! Instead, they were accompanied by an entire team of young boys who were busy playing football. Surprisingly, the Samson boys had convinced their parents to take all the kids along and they had to give in. After all, a smile from their kids is what parents want!

The only thing that the Samson couple did that day, at the picnic spot, was to act as spectators, occasionally cheering for the boys, all of whom were for the most part indifferent. They came to the couple every few minutes but just for water and refreshments. The loneliness that inevitably accompanies the uncertain behaviour of growing teenagers had hit them quite hard.

"Later also we tried planning outings on different occasions but the kids hardly ever agreed to come along," Mrs Samson said in a tired tone.

Laila thought to herself, "Maybe this extravagant city life makes way for such characteristic teenage issues. The limited resources and the restrictiveness of village life exposes children to economic hardships and responsibilities early on."

What the parents had considered as enjoyment turned out to be boring for the kids. Eventually, the couple made peace with this way of life, as they understood that it was the same for all parents with teenage kids.

After returning home, that very evening, while she was preparing dinner, Laila was suddenly reminded of the necklace that Mrs Samson had given to Nina for the party. Without wasting another moment, she called Nina who was completing a reading assignment in their room on the second floor. Nina came and asked, "What happened? Why have you called me so early? There's still some time for dinner."

A visibly uneasy Laila interrupted her and asked if she had returned the necklace. Nina had never been a careless child because her circumstances had made her wise beyond her years. She also realised that she should have returned the necklace by then. She replied, "I am sorry, I'll just get it from upstairs," and she rushed out.

Laila cautioned her, "Don't run, be careful."

Nina returned after about five minutes with the necklace and a pack of chocolates in her hand. She knocked on the bedroom door, went in, and gave both to Mrs Samson. She knew that the old lady was very fond of chocolates, and it was her way of showing that she was grateful.

Mrs Samson stared at the pack of chocolates deep in thought. Lending her necklace to Nina was a very small thing for Mrs Samson, but Nina's touching gesture said so much about her upbringing. That very moment, Mrs Samson finalized Nina's gift for her sixteenth birthday although there were still two years to go.

As kids grow up, emotional changes for them
Are more like high and low tides,
But for parents they aren't
Any less than dreaded roller-coaster rides.

05

The Roof Lays the Foundation

Laila had been working since she was eighteen years old. She never had the chance to enrol in college, but wished to realize her dream of graduating someday. Whenever she saw young girls in the neighbourhood heading to the office in the morning, she said to herself, "I wish I could have studied further."

One day, when she was ironing Mrs Samson's clothes, the old lady enquired, "Have you asked Nina about her plans for higher studies? What does she want to pursue as a career? I know she has a lot of interest in the sciences."

"She wants to be a nurse, Madam. Actually, it sort of runs in our genes. Our grandmother was a midwife, my mother wanted to be a paramedic. She was married off at a very young age and faced many economic challenges so she could not complete her studies. She always wanted me to be a nurse, but destiny had different plans for me too. I, however, want to make sure that Nina doesn't face any economic crunch on the road to a career of her choice."

Mrs Samson appreciated Laila's feelings and went on to ask, "Have you ever thought of pursuing higher studies since you came to Delhi? I know you've been working but did the thought cross your mind, ever?"

Laila smiled and said, "No, even if I want to, I know it is a distant reality. Earlier, I had the task of earning a living, but now, I also have to take care of Nina and her education. I guess it's too late now!"

Mrs Samson could see the tears that Laila tried to hide from her. Her uneasiness was revealed in her body language. Mrs Samson said to her, "My dear child, you are yet to see the strength that I can see in you. I'm sure, God has something great in store for you. Smile and life shall surely smile back."

Mrs Samson had a friend, Mrs Lalitha, whose house was within walking distance from hers. They often met and chatted over a cup of tea or coffee. On one such evening, while sipping hot coffee, Mrs Samson discussed this matter with her. Mrs Lalitha, who had retired from the administrative department of a university, suggested that Laila could at least pursue a correspondence course in her area of interest. Mrs Samson's face lit up and she got very excited.

That very day, she passed on the idea to Laila, who thanked her for thinking so deeply about her. However, the old lady saw that her excitement hadn't produced the desired results. She didn't want to thrust her idea upon Laila, so she left the decision completely up to the young girl.

That night, Laila got an unexpected call from her village. Due to unruly weather – strong winds and heavy rainfall, a part of the roof of their house had been blown off, and it needed immediate repairs. She became very anxious. She didn't have many belongings back there, but the repair work was unavoidable. Laila estimated that whatever work was to be done, would require at least a week-long trip. Nina had her exams, and Laila couldn't figure any way out.

Early the next morning, she called a couple of distant relatives and asked them if they could help. A few of her maternal aunts resided in her village. She tried hard to figure out a solution but to no avail. Then, she apprised Mrs Samson of the situation who suggested, "You should go to the village and resolve things as soon as possible. While you are away, Nina can stay with me on the ground floor." They decided to ask Sarita to stay over for a week to do the housework. This relieved Laila's anxiety to some extent.

Laila then rang up Raju to convey the same to him. Raju's phone was busy and the call couldn't be connected despite repeated attempts. Actually, he had taken a day off to take care of some personal paperwork at the bank. In the evening, when he returned home, he seemed very tense!

He told Mrs Samson that on his way back, he was informed by Sarita that Harsh was very unwell. Sarita got the child admitted to a nearby health facility, as he was severely dehydrated. Thus, Raju needed to rush home. Suddenly, everything became complicated, and Laila started feeling dizzy due to the build-up of anxiety.

Mrs Samson told Raju to leave for his home immediately. She calmed Laila down. She was soon reminded of Ron. Although Laila had mentioned about him only occasionally, the old lady knew that they talked once in a while on the phone. Since they were from the same village, Mrs Samson was sure that he'd be able to help Laila out. She told Laila to call him. Laila tried his number but couldn't get through to him. After an hour, she got a call from Ron and explained the situation to him.

Back there in the village, Ron had two younger siblings. He assured Laila that he'd call his brother right away and they'd do whatever they could to help her. This was a major breather for her. Although she was not completely at peace, she was able to catch some sleep that night.

By the next afternoon, Ron's brother had taken over the charge of the repair works at Laila's place, and when Ron informed her, this poor girl's joy knew no bounds. She thanked him profusely, and a few days later, when the work was over, she even called Ron's younger brother to express her gratitude.

Mrs Samson, with age, had developed an exceptional eye for detail. She had watched Laila very closely during this stressful time. It was not that sparks of love were flying all around, but she definitely sensed something and smiled at the evolving fondness between the childhood friends – Laila and Ron.

Later that evening, Raju also informed Mrs Samson that his son was stable and they had brought him back home. Finally, this tough span of time filled with terrible anxiety ended on a peaceful note, as things settled down with fruitful results.

Problems come and go;
Look for the seeds of strength that they sow!

06

A Hair-Raising Beginning to The New Year

A few uneventful months passed by until it was New Year's Eve; Laila was watering the plants, as she did every day, when she heard a thud-like sound accompanied by screams from Mrs Samson's room. A stunned Laila ran to check on Mrs Samson, and as soon as she opened the door, she shuddered with fear. Buddy and Brown, who were playing on the lawn, also ran inside. The scene was terrifying! The ceiling fan lay on the bed with Mrs Samson's foot under one of the blades; the old lady was scared stiff.

Mrs Samson said, "Laila, save me!" Laila swiftly got into action. Pushing the fan's blade away, she first helped Mrs Samson sit up and then calmed her down. The old lady held on to Laila like a small, terrified child. Thankfully, she didn't get injured owing to the shock-absorbing protection from the quilt.

Mrs Samson complained, "My ankle is paining. I think it is fractured!" Laila checked her ankle and said, "Madam, there is no swelling. I can just see some redness around the ankle. I will put an ice pack and it should be fine."

The old lady said, "No, please apply a pain relief ointment. The pain is unbearable." Laila did just that and she also bandaged Mrs Samson's ankle on her insistence. It was the shock effect that had made Mrs Samson scream out of nervousness; she perceived to have suffered a grave injury.

It was New Year's Day the next morning. All of them warmly greeted each other. The old lady was still in a bit of a shock and it was evident in the way she walked around the house, avoiding the path below the fans. By noon, she had overcome her fear and returned to normal.

Interestingly, a few years ago, when Mrs Samson had adopted Brown and Buddy, she had decided to celebrate the duo's birthday on this day. It was time for a double celebration in the Samson household. This helped in bringing about the required change in her mood.

Raju and Laila transported the canines by car to a pet salon, as desired by Mrs Samson, for a pampering session. Buddy was more docile and frail compared to Brown although they were brothers. Actually, Buddy had a leg deformity since birth and limped. Brown wasn't necessarily aggressive but he was somewhat more active.

Their session at the salon lasted for a good three hours. When it was time to return home, they gave Laila and Raju a real tough time. Both enjoyed the grooming and pampering so much that they were not ready to head back. They ran around and jumped in the play area which had balls, toys, treats, and other attractive items for pets. Brown even picked up a fight with a Chow-Chow puppy in the play area. This intimidated Buddy to such an extent that he started crying. Finally, the handlers had to intervene to separate the two of them.

Anyhow, after letting them play for some extra time, Laila and Raju managed to bring them home. In the evening, Nina got some balloons for them and assembled a cake from the dog food kept at home. Later, all of them played with Brown and Buddy, starting off their new year on a celebratory note.

A week into the new year, Mrs Samson's younger son, Roger, arrived with his family to stay with her for a week. They were on a world tour, so they were going to stay in Delhi for a short while only. It was a super-busy week as relatives came over to meet them. Several shopping trips were lined up and they made sure to include Mrs Samson in everything that they did. Mrs Samson had a soft corner for her younger daughter-in-law, Irene. They used to talk on the phone almost every other day and were more like friends.

When the children left, Mrs Samson felt really low for a couple of days. Then, one day, she fell unconscious. Luckily, Laila was sitting just next to her and patted her swiftly, prompting Mrs Samson to regain consciousness. This was the first time that such a situation had cropped up. They felt that it might be due to weakness, as the past week had been very hectic for her.

A few weeks later, it happened again, and this time when she regained consciousness, her reflexes were slow. Laila alerted Raju, and they both felt the need to take her to the hospital. When they reached the emergency and the doctors performed some tests, a low sugar level was ascertained to be the cause of her sudden illness. Although her blood glucose levels had returned to normal, she was told that she would need monitoring on a regular basis.

When all three of them returned home, the gate was bolted from the outside. Laila looked for Nina in the vicinity but she was nowhere to be found. Buddy could be heard barking incessantly on the lawn. Laila felt her heart in her mouth. She thought, "Nina never steps out of the house without telling me. Nina, where are you? I hope you are safe."

Laila opened the gate and took Mrs Samson inside towards the living room and told Raju about Nina's disappearance. Raju parked the car and went searching for both of them. He first rushed to Nina's friend's place in the neighbourhood but to no avail. Then, he asked all the neighbours, but none of them had any clue. He hurriedly started walking towards the local market thinking that Nina may have gone there to get something.

Raju had just reached halfway when he saw Nina running and screaming along the sidewalk. She was looking for Brown. Raju shouted, sprinted, and managed to reach her. Immediately, he realised that Brown was missing. He asked her, "Why did you take Brown out all by yourself?"

She was out of breath but replied, "I didn't, I was inside when I heard Buddy. When I came out, the gate was open and Brown wasn't there." Raju then told her to go back home saying that he would continue to look for Brown. After an hour, Raju also returned but without Brown.

Mrs Samson was crying and so was Nina. Laila was trying to calm both of them down. She told Raju, "You stay here. I'll go and look for Brown and I'll take Buddy with me. Maybe he can guide us."

Soon after Laila left, Nina's friend came with her parents asking about her wellbeing. When they were told about the situation, the father said, "I saw Brown playing with children in the society park some time ago." Raju sprang up from the chair and ran towards the gate. He was about to reach the gate when Laila entered. She was holding Buddy's leash in one hand and Brown's in the other.

Yes, she had finally found Brown! She told everyone that some children, who were playing in the colony, had found the gate open and had innocently decided to take him to the park. It was Buddy who led her there, and she found Brown playing with the children, unaware of the trauma he had caused his family! Mrs Samson heaved a sigh of relief and so did Nina. Both of them cuddled Brown and weren't ready to let go of him. So much attention got him irritated, and he then ran away to play with Buddy in their kennel in the lawn.

Proximity to loved ones gives joy and positivity,
And distances can numb you emotionally.
Fear of losing someone, on the other hand,
May altogether, blow out one's sense of security.

07

The Wedding Invitation

It was springtime, and there was a riot of colours in the garden. Flowers blossomed, and butterflies and honeybees visited the flowers and enlivened the fauna. Mrs Samson loved red roses, and she had three healthy rose bushes in her garden. She made sure that Laila did the pruning timely. This was partly why they had healthy and fragrant flowers.

One day, Nina spotted an unusual creature on the pavement that led up to the gate. It slithered away so fast that the child could just get a glimpse of it. She went inside and explained this to Mrs Samson. "DG, I just saw a very tiny snake-like thing on the lawn. It was very shiny and half of its body was red. But it was extremely swift and moved in a strange, zig-zag manner. Have you ever seen something like this?"

Mrs Samson understood that Nina must have spotted a Red-tailed skink and explained to her that it was commonly found in gardens. She also told her to be careful and not to go near it. Nina was very fascinated by Chameleons, and Laila had to constantly remind her to stay away from them in the garden. So, Mrs Samson thought it wise to caution Nina beforehand.

The same noon, Laila got a call from Ron. Generally, he would call in the evening. Therefore, when Laila saw the incoming call, she was a little worried. Fortunately, everything was fine and he told her that his sister, Rita, was going to get married in a month. The wedding was to take place in the village.

He said, "I am so excited and happy to share this news with you. Rita is getting married, and I want you and Nina to be a part of the celebration."

"That's great news. Congratulations to all of you. I am sure uncle and aunty will be super excited too. Thanks for the invitation, Ron. I'll have to ask Mrs Samson about it."

"I am sure Mrs Samson won't have a problem with you taking some time off."

Laila also thought likewise and said, "Yes, but I'll still have to ask her. And I'm afraid I won't be able to bring Nina along because she will be having her annual exams."

The conversation went on for a while as Ron told her about how the marriage had been fixed, and Laila enjoyed listening to it all.

Laila took a couple of days just to decide if she would ask Mrs Samson about the trip to her village. Actually, there were a few reasons for her hesitation. First, Mrs Samson was dependent on Laila for her daily chores. Second, she wasn't sure if she could leave Nina unattended during her exam time. Third, she had never been close to Rita such that her presence or absence would make a difference to Rita or her family. The only reason in favour of the visit was that Ron was a friend and he had always been there whenever she needed him since the time her mother had passed away. Thus, she wished to honour his invitation.

Just when she decided to ask Mrs Samson, the phone rang and the operator on the other side called for Mrs Samson. She was informed that due to some pending essential documentation, she would be required to visit the bank in two business days or else all her transactions would be halted. No doubt, old age brings along insecurities and sometimes logical explanations fall short when it comes to feeling convinced. The same happened with the old lady. She got extremely anxious and had it not been late in the day, she would have rushed to the bank that very moment.

Laila knew that it was going to be an unnecessarily anxious night for Mrs Samson. She tried her best and arranged all the papers in an effort to comfort Mrs Samson. Both Raju and Laila told her that there was no need to worry and that they would take her to the bank at the earliest in the morning, but she became really tense. Laila had no option but to connect Mrs Samson to Irene, her younger daughter-in-law, who finally calmed her down. Still, the lady slept for three hours only and so did Laila, because whenever anxious, Mrs Samson developed pains and aches.

The next morning, after breakfast, they went to the bank. Although it took a couple of hours, all formalities were completed well in time. When they returned home, it was lunchtime. Nina had also reached home after writing her exam. Laila had prepared scrumptious pasta and garlic bread which they all enjoyed. Mrs Samson was a true foodie at heart. She would tell Laila to keep learning new recipes from cookbooks and cookery shows so that all of them could enjoy a variety of cuisines from the comfort of their home.

After lunch, she asked Laila, "Where is my sugar-free brownie sundae? I thought we were having it for dessert today!"

Laila, who was somewhat lost due to the dilemma about the trip to the village, said, "Oh, I'm sorry, I completely forgot. I'll just get it."

"You forgot my cashews too!" Mrs Samson said. By now she had sensed that something was amiss.

Later in the afternoon, Laila decided to discuss the matter with Mrs Samson. When she explained the situation and asked for Mrs Samson's opinion, the old lady replied, "If I were you, I wouldn't attend the wedding."

Laila had got her answer, and half-heartedly accepted it saying, "I think you are right, Thanks." Then she turned around and started walking towards the kitchen.

Seconds later, in a naughty tone, Mrs Samson said, "Of course not! You must go to the wedding. You'll get a chance to meet everyone back there, have a look at your house too and then return back to the city. We'll manage things over here. Now go and take rest. It's been a long day." Her tone conveyed that she had sealed the deal. She didn't want Laila to think more about it and she surely didn't want her to miss the trip.

Laila had always been very committed to her duties towards Mrs Samson, and extremely responsible as far as Nina was concerned. In her mind, she still had doubts about going to the wedding. The next morning, surprisingly, she got a call from Rita, requesting her to be there for the wedding. The warm invite made Laila decide in favour of attending the celebration.

Ron called the day after, to know about Laila's decision. He was happy to know that she would be coming to the wedding. He shared his plans with her saying, "My leave has been sanctioned. I plan to reach Delhi first and then

I'll pick you up, following which we'll catch the next train to Dehradun. After the wedding, both of us will head back to Delhi and then I'll proceed further to my duty station." She agreed and conveyed the same to Mrs Samson.

Thinking, re-thinking and planning
Is all that we, as humans, can do.
The route, I guess, is already planned,
Also, how and when to go through!

08

An Enjoyable Trip

A few more days went by, and it was time for Laila to pack her bags and leave for Dehradun to attend Rita's wedding. Nina gave her some letters and candies for her friends with whom she had lost touch when she moved to Delhi. Little Nina's benevolence was definitely worth some appreciation. Mrs Samson gifted Laila a beautiful saree and also lent her a pink pearl necklace set to wear for the wedding. Laila felt very shy accepting the gift. However, Mrs Samson's motherly talk compelled her to agree.

Laila was all set, and Sarita was back with baby Harsh at Mrs Samson's house. It was almost time for Ron to arrive, and Mrs Samson was eagerly waiting to meet him. Although she didn't express anything outwardly, there was definitely something in her mind regarding Laila's future.

Laila on the other hand, still hadn't moved an inch from thinking about anything beyond childhood friendship! Despite her reluctance, Mrs Samson ensured that Laila prepared some snacks which they could take along for the train journey. Maybe she wanted Ron to notice Laila's cooking skills!

A few moments later, a tall, young man entered. "Good afternoon, Madam. I'm Ronit. How are you doing?" asked Ron as he stepped into the living room. He was dressed in semi-formal attire. With shoulders pulled back, an erect posture, and a perfect stride, he completely fitted into the gentleman-frame that Mrs Samson had in mind.

"I'm very well. How are you, Ron? Have a seat. By the way, I already know that you prefer to be addressed as Ron," said Mrs Samson with a smile.

An introductory talk ensued and then she asked him about his family and siblings. She was eager to know what had motivated him to join the defence forces. He elaborated, "Madam, I was born and brought up in a village in Chakrata, Dehradun. And since the Army has a very prestigious institute in the state, we grew up amidst inspirational news and talks about the defence forces. In my formative years, I often saw soldiers in neighbouring areas. There is an unmatched sense of pride and satisfaction attached to serving the nation. Also, my father always motivated me to join the forces."

Mrs Samson was happy to gain some insight into Ron's upbringing. Her interaction with Ron was evident of her motherly concern for Laila.

During the course of the conversation, Laila and Ron also shared a couple of their childhood experiences which were so hilarious that Mrs Samson had to stop both of them midway; her jaws had started to pain from the continuous laughter. Meanwhile, Nina sat next to Laila, and resting her head on Laila's lap, she said, "I will miss you, come back soon. Had it not been exam time, I would have accompanied you!"

Laila caressed her and said, "But then, who will take special care of Mrs Samson, just like you do! You're a big girl now. I'm sure you'll manage everything. Study well for your exams."

When it was time for them to leave, Mrs Samson and Nina wished them a happy and safe journey. Brown and Buddy also showered Laila with lots of affection, excitedly wagging their tails as she walked towards the gate. She told them affectionately, "Sarita Aunty and Nina will take good care of you while I'm away, my lovelies!"

Once she was seated in the train, Laila called home to inform them that they were en route. For a couple of hours, Nina had become so engrossed playing with Harsh that she didn't feel Laila's absence. Only when Mrs Samson reminded her of her studies did she start missing her elder sister! Kids, after all, are like that. That night, Mrs Samson told Nina, "You sleep next to me, and Sarita Aunty and Harsh can sleep in your room on the second floor." She wanted to ensure that Nina slept well and woke up on time for her exam.

The following morning, Laila called to inform them that she had reached home safely and Ron's brother had already arranged for the essential groceries for her.

The wedding functions were to commence the next afternoon. In the meantime, she had to wind up some paperwork at the bank's branch in the village and clear some pending household bills. Later in the evening, Nina told her that her exam had gone well and she had started preparing for the next one which was scheduled for the day after.

The next day, Laila went to meet some of her neighbours. She also passed on the stuff that Nina had sent for her old friends. She bought a box of sweets and went to Ron's place to attend Rita's engagement ceremony.

She was excited to meet all of Ron's relatives. She had met many of them in childhood but had since lost touch. Ron introduced her to Rita's fiancé who was from one of the neighbouring states and was employed at a bank.

It was a warm family get-together, and it was then that Laila started to acknowledge the special treatment that was being given to her. Rita danced her heart out with Laila as if they had been friends for years. Not for a moment did Laila feel like a guest. It was an enjoyable afternoon with songs, dances, great food, family fun, and celebration. Later in the evening, Laila helped them wrap up all the gifts for the groom's side and also assisted Ron with the decorations.

At night, a tired Laila called Nina to enquire about the wellbeing of all of them in Delhi and then she went to sleep. Early the next morning, she went to Ron's house, as she had promised Rita that she would help her with her hair and makeup for the wedding. She had, indeed, brought an elaborate makeup kit from Delhi as Rita's wedding gift. Then, all of them got ready and proceeded to the wedding venue.

Laila was one of the bridesmaids and she enjoyed every bit of the event. The wedding ceremony went as planned. Then, it was time for Rita to leave with the groom. The family members had tears in their eyes and so did Rita. Everyone blessed her and wished the newlyweds the very best. Laila had always known Ron to be a strong man. However, when his sister was on the verge of leaving, Laila could see the tears that he tried to conceal. He took a few moments to regain composure after she left. Then he got busy with settling all the bills of the caterers, decorators, etc.

Laila returned to her home as she had to meet a couple of her relatives in a neighbouring village. Later that night, she packed her belongings as they had to leave the next morning. Ron picked her up from her home and they boarded the train to Delhi. It had been a very busy, rushed trip for them. It was then that they got some free time to talk.

Ron started off by asking, "What are your future plans, Laila?"

"I have loads of responsibilities and they are going to keep me occupied for another decade. There is no scope for any new plans."

"Come on. You are a strong girl, and I'm sure you can manage everything."

"I must say, Mrs Samson is a great lady. I respect her and am indebted to her for what she has done for me and Nina. Who takes on the responsibility of two young girls these days? We are safe with her and she provides for us. The only way I can pay her back is to offer her the best possible care."

"That's true, Laila!"

"Nina is also growing up and will soon start going to college. I want her to have a stable, well-paying job one day. In another five to seven years, I will have to plan for Nina's marriage and so on and so forth. So, several events and changes are already lined up and I practically have no scope for any personal transitions."

Although Ron saw little scope for a relationship based on what he was being told, he gathered that there was no one else on her mind with respect to an alliance. He thought that it would be wise to leave the topic at that because he didn't want to stir up any emotional turmoil in Laila's mind. He understood her state very well and wanted her to feel secure under the umbrella of their friendship.

"I've been going on and on about myself, you tell me… what are your plans?"

He simply said, "I want to focus on my career. I want to be an officer one day and I must work wholeheartedly towards that. Everything else can wait." Before Laila could probe further, breakfast was served. And their focus shifted to the freshness of the cutlets that accompanied the fragrant tea and bread. Laila loved the cutlets although Ron found them to be too spicy.

Ron went on to explain to Laila about the disciplined life of soldiers in the forces, the facilities, the fitness regimens, the aura, etc. Laila seemed fascinated and enjoyed the conversation. The beautiful journey then ended when their train reached Delhi.

Mrs Samson had sent Raju to pick Laila up from the train station. They bid goodbye to each other and Laila thanked him for treating her like family. With a wish to meet more often, both of them, smilingly, went their own way.

Quantification of love and care
Has never been a real thing;
A tie can last beyond a lifetime,
If joy, security and satisfaction it can bring.

09

Laila on a Sticky Wicket

A year passed by and Nina was going to turn sixteen that September. She had been telling Laila for the past six months that for this birthday, she wanted to give a treat to a few friends at a cafe. Most of her peers had celebrated their sixteenth birthday the same way. Birthdays were generally celebrated by distributing sweets to one's classmates. But turning sixteen was special. Thankfully, Nina was studying at a government school, and hence, Laila was spared the pain of numerous extravagant wishes. She knew very well that children at public schools in those days followed the trend of birthday celebrations at restaurants, hotels, and party halls. Thus, Laila promised to fulfil this wish of hers.

Unaware of the agreement between Nina and Laila, Mrs Samson was also planning a birthday celebration for Nina at home. One day, she talked to Laila about it. The extreme excitement with which she had explained her plan, prevented Laila from telling her about Nina's wish. She, however, said to Mrs Samson, "Madam, I think we should keep it simple and sweet like we always do. I'm sure Nina will be very happy with that. Don't pamper her too much. I don't want her to develop high expectations regarding her birthday celebrations in the coming years. I can't afford such luxuries!"

"You don't have to bother about that! Her DG will take care of everything. She is like a grandchild to me.

You can't stop me from showering love on her. She is such a disciplined and sweet child. Don't ever say that again!" Mrs Samson said in an irked manner. She became breathless while speaking, so Laila rubbed her palms, pacified her, and told her to relax.

Now, Laila was in a dilemma. On the one hand, she wanted to keep her promise of a small celebration at a cafe. On the other hand, she was obligated to honour Mrs Samson's wish which also meant that she'd have to forget about Nina's desire for an outdoor celebration.

Somewhere deep inside, Laila knew that such seemingly frivolous teenage wishes have a small yet significant impact on the confidence of youngsters. She had given up on her own desires when she was Nina's age, because of numerous constraints. This prompted her to try and accommodate Nina's cherished wish, anyway.

The whole day, such thoughts kept her mind occupied. In the evening, she talked to Nina about it. On hearing Mrs Samson's plan, Nina expressed subtle resentment saying, "It is my birthday, and you made a promise to me a long time back. I don't want to celebrate it at home. I've already told my friends. Now, I don't want to back out. Most of the children in my class celebrated their sixteenth birthday in a similar way," she said, tearing up.

Laila's heart broke, because she felt pressure from both sides. She hugged Nina and told her, "Don't worry, stop crying. We'll celebrate it the way you want to. Now, give me a smile, my sweetheart!"

Moments later, Laila took Brown and Buddy out for their walk, and Nina went to the park to play. At dinner time, Nina asked Laila, "Have you told DG about the celebration at the cafe?"

Laila calmed her down by saying, "It is night time and Mrs Samson should not be disturbed, so I will talk to her in the morning. You don't worry."

The next day, when Nina came back from school, Mrs Samson was eagerly waiting for her with a gift. Actually, with just a day left for Nina's birthday, she couldn't contain her excitement, so she wanted to give Nina her gift in advance. When Nina opened her gift, her eyes lit up. It was a delicate beaded charm bracelet. But as soon as Mrs Samson told her that she wanted her to wear it for the grand celebration at home, Nina's excitement receded like a tide in the ocean.

She looked towards Laila who signalled her to stay silent for the moment. "DG, I'm full. I ate in the canteen today," she told Mrs Samson and went to her room.

Laila understood that Nina was upset and decided to talk to Mrs Samson about it. She then explained the whole situation to Mrs Samson who patiently listened, as she was a lady of ripe experience and didn't want the child to be unhappy. Laila felt sad to see the old lady's zeal fizzle out, but this time she had to be Nina's advocate. She was the only one among them who had a neutral view of the generation gap.

However, a graceful Mrs Samson gave in to the child's wish. She said, "Now I understand why you had tried to convince me to have a low-key celebration yesterday! You've started hiding things from me, Laila."

A visibly disturbed and embarrassed Laila thought it wise to keep quiet in order to let the sentiments settle.

She didn't mean to hurt either of them. She knew that Mrs Samson would eventually understand her situation, a little later, if not right away.

Next, it was party time. An eclectic spread of pizzas, a blueberry cake at the centre, milkshakes in attractive tall glasses, and birthday tiaras were the main attraction in a cosy corner of the cafe's terrace where Nina's birthday was to be celebrated. Five of Nina's friends had arrived and three were on their way. Nina wore a beautiful lavender-coloured calf-length dress that Laila had gifted to her for her birthday. It wasn't a boutique dress though. Laila had got it stitched from a tailor in the vicinity. Nina excitedly accessorized it with the bracelet that was gifted by Mrs Samson.

On one of the side tables, there were return gifts for the girls. Laila and Nina had specially curated small gift baskets with hair accessories and candies as return gifts. When all the girls arrived, it was time for the cake cutting. Laila lit the candles, Nina made a wish and the girls clapped and sang the birthday song. Although Nina was going to cut a cake at home too, Laila connected with Mrs Samson on video call so that she could also be a part of this celebration.

A few other tables were also occupied by that time. So, everybody clapped and joined in the cake-cutting ceremony. Nina was ecstatic. She enjoyed the snacks with all her friends. Laila clicked lots of pictures and when the party was over, she and Nina thanked all the girls for coming and gave them their return gifts.

After about an hour, they reached home. Raju had arranged for balloons, cake, and pink flowers on Mrs

Samson's order. She wanted to surprise Nina with celebratory decorations and make her feel special. When Nina saw all of it, she ran straight to her and gave her a tight hug. Later, she thanked her lovely DG for understanding and allowing her to celebrate at the cafe with her friends. Mrs Samson smilingly blessed her, and then they all had dinner and slept.

What is an intermediate generation
If not the lettuce leaf
That's pressed firmly between
The elder and younger piece of the bun!

10

Nina Falls and Rises Thereafter

Almost twelve uneventful months passed by. Things were on track as far as Nina's studies were concerned. Laila still hadn't decided on pursuing further studies. Ron had his eyes set on becoming an officer in the forces. He was trying to clear an entrance exam that would allow him a lateral entry after the completion of a specialised course.

Back in the Samson household, it was a bright day; Brown and Buddy were lazing around in the lawn while Mrs Samson sat in her rocking chair, sipping her favourite drink, coffee. She liked hers with a hint of sugar, lots of milk, and garnished with some chocolate shavings on top. Generally, she had a sandwich or maybe a raspberry-jam bar to go with it. However, on this day, she was full and skipped the accompaniments. She felt a bit weak too.

Laila came to the lawn after cleaning the kitchen. She asked, "Have you finished your coffee, Madam? Do you feel like eating a cookie or are you done?"

Mrs Samson shook her head and said, "No, my child! I don't feel like having anything." She handed over the coffee mug to Laila. Raju was busy giving the car a thorough wash in the parking lot.

Mrs Samson had to attend a small party at her friend's place. There were still a couple of hours before she was to leave, so she decided to take a half-hour nap. She told Laila, "I think I'll wear the pink silk shirt with fawn trousers. They might need a bit of ironing. Please do that for me and wake me up in time." Laila did the needful, and later she got ready and they left for the party.

The get-together was organised to celebrate the graduation of her friend's grandson. Laila had been with Mrs Samson for so long that by then, she got along very well with most of the other old ladies and their caretakers. That day, one of the ladies asked Laila about her future plans, marriage and all. Laila tried to dodge the questions politely. As soon as Mrs Samson realised that Laila was a bit uncomfortable, she chided her friend, "Let the young girls enjoy themselves. They hardly get to meet. You can talk about this some other time. Now, pay attention to your cards, otherwise, we'll lose the game!"

After spending about two hours there, they returned home. Nina was also back from school and was studying, while Brown and Buddy were asleep in their kennel. It was Nina's last year at school and she was exceptionally busy with her studies. She wanted to give it her best and aspired to join a premier nursing college in Delhi.

Later that evening, Mrs Samson suddenly complained of chest pain which sent Laila and Nina into a spin. Laila wanted to take her to the doctor but the old lady rejected her idea saying, "It is just heartburn and nothing else. Maybe it is due to the food that was served at the party today." She took an over-the-counter antacid and told Laila to relax. Laila, on the other hand, became anxious and called Irene, as she usually did in such situations. Irene talked to Mrs Samson but even she couldn't convince her mother-in-law to see a doctor. She told Laila to try giving some caraway seeds which they often used as a home remedy for acidity.

After about an hour, Mrs Samson's pain went away. She told Laila, "See, I was right. It was just acidity and heartburn. Give me a cup of yoghurt and that'll be my dinner." Laila thought to herself, "Just heartburn for you and no less than a heart attack for me!"

It was 8:00 p.m. and Mrs Samson had retired to her room when a scream was heard along with a noise as if something had fallen down the stairs. Laila rushed outside to see what it was and got the shock of her life. She found Nina lying on the floor, writhing in pain. The child had slipped down the stairs. It was an emergency and they rushed her to the hospital. Unfortunately, Nina had fractured her right arm.

The doctor had to put a cast on her arm for six weeks. He gave her painkillers as she was in tremendous pain. She lamented, "I have my examinations in three months. How will I study?" The situation added to her woes. She was fearful and couldn't stop her tears. After all, it was her right arm.

Laila consoled her. "Nina, the first week may be difficult, but after that, you will see some improvement. Drink milk twice a day and you'll get better soon. Till then, I promise to give you all of my time and attention."

The following day, Nina didn't go to school, as her body was still recovering from the fall. She felt low, and both Mrs Samson and Laila tried their best to change her frame of mind. Brown and Buddy also followed her everywhere, sniffing her cast again and again. Unable to use her right arm, the poor child was completely at sea.

Over the next few days, Nina figured out how to use her arm while putting the least strain on it. Her friends were also helping her at school. Time passed and her cast was finally removed after six weeks. Everyone was relieved to know that the fracture had healed, and thankful for the fact that she didn't need the cast anymore.

One day, Rita called Laila to inform her that she was visiting Delhi with her husband and asked if they could meet. Laila readily agreed. She had thoroughly enjoyed her previous interaction with Rita at her wedding.

Nina was having her exams. As decided, one day, while Laila waited outside the exam centre, Rita and her husband came to meet her. They spent some time over a cup of coffee at a nearby cafe and chatted freely. Rita wanted to know more about Laila, for obvious reasons! They talked about their childhood and then about the build-up of responsibilities on each side. She really appreciated the way Laila was handling everything that life threw at her. It was an enjoyable talk as was evident from their expressions. Then, Rita and her husband left for Goa which was their next destination.

Three months went by and it was Nina's results-declaration day. Her school results had been declared a month ago and she had performed really well in her exams. That day, the results for the nursing college entrance exam were to be declared.

Nina was a bit nervous but confident that she would make it through. At noon, when she sat in front of the computer at a cyber cafe with Laila standing behind her, she screamed out of joy and jumped out of her seat. Both of them hugged each other tightly and Laila had tears in her eyes. Nina had not only cleared the exam but also scored the highest marks! Her efforts had paid off.

An emotional Laila said, "I'm so proud of you. Your journey starts from here. I'm even happier because you will be getting a full scholarship for your studies. Everything you achieve will be solely based on your ability. Embark confidently on your journey and be proud of yourself. This is what I call being self-made." She then kissed her little sister on the forehead.

Once the desire to rise starts fuelling your flight,
Hurdles can be overcome and the future becomes bright.

11

A Tale of Accomplishments

Nina joined college and had since shifted to the hostel. She visited occasionally on the weekends or during holidays. She had started enjoying her course very much; it was evident from her performance in the first semester. Often, when she came home, Mrs Samson discussed minor health issues with her, asking her for health tips.

Ron, on the other hand, put in his best effort and cleared the entrance examination. It was a much-awaited milestone for him. He was ecstatic and so were his family members. Laila had been instrumental in motivating him to keep trying till he got through. So, she was even happier for him.

Laila had more time for herself after Nina went away to college. One day, Mrs Samson again broached the topic of pursuing a correspondence degree with her. Since Laila had more time to spare, and her financial responsibilities had also been reduced, she decided to give it a serious thought.

With Mrs Lalitha's help, a month later, Laila joined a diploma certificate course. She was returning to her studies after a long gap. The day her books arrived, she became really excited. She eagerly flipped through the pages and decided on the topics that she'd cover first. She bought some stationery and arranged it neatly along with her books on the study table that Nina had been using.

After the initial week, she got extremely busy with household chores because Mrs Samson's friend was coming with her daughter to stay for a week. She was a naturalized American citizen and was visiting Delhi for a month. First, the preparations ate into much of Laila's time. Later, with guests at home, there was no scope for studies. However, Laila was always clear that work was her priority. She made plans to study long hours at night. Once the guests had left, she worked on her plans.

In the following months, there were days when she couldn't study at all. She would cry when she picked up her dust-covered books after long gaps. One day she told Ron, "I won't be able to sit for my exams. With just a week left, I haven't even started my revision. I shouldn't have enrolled for the course. I could have saved money for Nina instead of paying the course fee!"

"Are you crazy? Your pessimistic approach will ruin everything. How can you even think this way? If Nina gets to know about this, she will be mad at you," Ron admonished her.

Laila became emotional, and Ron realised that he had been too harsh with her. He softened his tone the next moment and said, "Laila, I'm sorry. Listen to me, please. You still have time. Don't give up at this stage. I'm sure you'll be able to do it. Don't bother about the results. Just give it your best shot."

Laila understood his point and resolved to study hard. When the results were out, she was somewhat satisfied with her performance. Later, she became more cautious about following her schedule.

By then, Nina had also completed two semesters at her nursing school. One day, there she was, on the stage, receiving an award for her exemplary performance! A proud and ecstatic Laila sat in the audience capturing the golden moment on her phone.

"Very intelligent child and you are such a young mother," said one of the ladies sitting next to her in the audience.

"Thanks. Actually, she's my sister," Laila said proudly.

"Oh, I see, I should have guessed," said the lady, smiling.

A beaming Nina came to Laila with her trophy and hugged her. Afterwards, Nina took the warden's permission to show Laila her room. They had some instant noodles and coffee, the staples found in every hostel room! Then Laila returned home as Nina was to make the trip home the day after.

That evening, Mrs Samson was glad to see the trophy. She authoritatively instructed Laila, "Put it in my room till Nina comes. Then she can take it upstairs." The old lady went on to elaborate on her own academic excellence saying, "Even I used to be among the top rankers at school. Actually, I was more of a bookworm." Laila had a hearty laugh.

Mrs Samson continued, "When I joined college, I decided that, unlike my school life, I would thoroughly enjoy college life. I wanted to have a balanced approach to studies and extra-curricular activities. The first year at college was great, and I wrote my exams with minimal stress."

"What an experience it must have been!" Laila exclaimed. Mrs Samson nodded. "I remember my parents often anxiously asking me about the result dates, seeing my casual attitude. Suddenly, during my vacation, my friend called to inform me that I had topped the institute! I was amazed."

"Oh! That must have been exciting!" Laila said.

"It sure was! But you know, soon it led me into the endless cycle of untiring hard work till I finished my degree. I had done well despite taking it easy. Later, I guess, my desire to maintain my rank in the following semesters overpowered my laid-back attitude."

Mrs Samson did not pursue a career for long because she had got married at an early age and chose to focus on her responsibilities rather than her ambitions. However, she maintained that she had enjoyed every phase of life and took pride in all her achievements.

We often wish to be blessed
With a sprinkle of the heavenly spray
Which can clear up the haze
And wipe all the struggles away;
Meanwhile, only sincere determination
Can prevent us from stopping midway!

12

Emotional Strings

Time went by, and it was Nina's last semester at college. Being a bright student, she applied and qualified for an on-site training program during her autumn break. It was at a nursing home nearby. By this time, Laila had also completed her correspondence course.

That year, when Ron visited Delhi, he brought a beautiful silk saree for Laila as her graduation gift. Laila was delighted to receive it.

"You are being partial. I am also graduating this year. Where is my gift?" asked Nina.

This left Mrs Samson in splits. "I'll get a gift for you when you graduate. Let your sister enjoy hers! Ron has brought such a beautiful sari for her. Even I'm a bit jealous!" she said.

"I'll get one for you too next time," Ron said smiling.

Later in the evening, when Ron had left, Laila tried the saree on. Mrs Samson and Nina playfully teased her, telling her that she was blushing. Laila shrugged off the teasing, and she went to change. By then, she began to acknowledge that there was a certain connect between her and Ron which was beyond friendship. However, she was clear that a commitment from her side was not possible. Ron, on the other hand, was undemanding and wished to preserve their relationship.

Laila believed that a gentleman like Ron deserved his share of companionship in life which she was unable to offer him. She had decided early on to dedicatedly serve Mrs Samson because of the motherly support that she had provided her in her hour of need. Laila never thought of getting married because she could neither leave the lady alone in her golden years nor could she trust someone else with Mrs Samson's care.

A few months later, Nina graduated from college and joined a government hospital as a trainee nurse. She was excited and performed her duties dedicatedly. Her seniors were appreciative of her work, and she often received commendation certificates.

One day, when she returned home, she was heartbroken and weepy. Laila got worried and asked her, "What's the matter? Why are you so sad?"

For the first time, Nina had seen a young man die in the emergency ward. "I was handling an accident case and due to intra-cranial injury, the patient could not be saved. His wife and three-year-old daughter were waiting outside the emergency room to hear some positive news. When informed about the loss, the woman fainted. Seeing the situation, the small child had to be whisked away. I handed her over to her relatives." Clearly, Nina had seen the toughest day at work and it had revived a few of her painful memories.

Laila somehow managed to calm her down while Mrs Samson reminded her that in her profession, she was going to encounter many such incidences. She just needed to do her best with every patient and leave the rest to God. She told Nina, "Just like God has sent Laila to take care of you, He has plans and angels for all His children."

Time flew by and Nina visited again five months later. Since she had started working, this was her second visit. She used to come home more often when in college. Now, with odd shifts, she had started staying at the hostel.

One day, when Laila was done cooking the afternoon meal, Mrs Samson told her to clean and reset the books on the shelf placed in the furthest corner of her room. They were the most precious ones from Mr Samson's collection of books. A few of them were signed copies from authors.

Mrs Samson was not a great fan of books, but every now and then, she would take a peek inside these special books to look at her husband's notes. Her husband had indeed been an avid reader all through his life. She would run her fingers over the handwritten notes and then touch her fingers to her lips as if to kiss them. Sometimes, tears welled up in her eyes. It was definitely a precious collection, so she made sure that Laila wiped them clean fortnightly.

While Laila was at her job, Nina entered the room. She sat beside Mrs Samson and began flipping through the pages of a book that seemed fascinating to her. The cover had the picture of a solitary rose on the verge of wilting. On one of its pages, there was a note from Mr Samson which read as follows:

Far you may be today,
But closer you'll be
By tomorrow;
What must I say?
All be lost if I wait,
Joy will turn into sorrow!

Nina's eyes were glued to this note. She read it over and over again but felt the need to go into deeper detail. She asked Mrs Samson about the note. Mrs Samson replied, "Your uncle, Mr Samson, generally advocated free and unbiased expression of deeper thoughts. During his university years, our elder son was reluctant to visit us. Instead, he wanted to visit Europe or some other place with his friends every year during vacation. This pained us because we were eager to meet him. However, we didn't want to pressurize him. It was during one of those emotional moments that Mr Samson penned this down."

When Nina heard this, she was deeply touched. "DG, some feelings are so complex that they unfold only with age, I guess," she said. She then put the book back in its tastefully customised transparent cover. With deep thoughts, she went for a stroll on the lawn. Nina had been struck by a certain reality! She realised that it was a timely signal for her to be more responsible towards Laila. Subsequently, she made it a point to stay home on the weekends at least twice a month.

Emotional clarity makes us who we are;
It brings words and actions at par.

13

Tough and Trying Times

Back in the village at Dehradun, Ron and his family were rejoicing. He had realized his dream of becoming an officer. He was now Lieutenant Ronit Sharma. It was a moment of pride, not just for the family but for the entire village. They took part in a special prayer held at a temple in the vicinity to express gratitude. Sweets were distributed and all the people showered their good wishes and blessings on Ron.

Mrs Samson called him up. "Hello, am I speaking to Lieutenant Sharma?" she asked.

Ron had a wide smile on his face. "Yes, Mrs Samson. It's Lieutenant Ronit Sharma here. How have you been?" Their joyous conversation lasted for about ten minutes after which Laila congratulated him once again. She was, of course, the first to know about it and they had already talked earlier.

Nina experienced similar sentiments. She had completed one year as a nurse. She had been constantly applying to super speciality hospitals as she wanted to gain experience and wide exposure. One day, she got an interview call from Hyderabad. It was from a prestigious medical college. She excitedly told Laila, "You won't believe it! I got a call from the best hospital in Hyderabad."

"I knew you'd get selected. Remember what I told you when you applied for this job?"

"Yes, you were positive about it right from the beginning!" replied Nina.

Soon, it was interview time. Laila accompanied her to Hyderabad. Her interview went smooth and she got selected. They told her to join as soon as possible. Both returned to Delhi where Nina was supposed to put in her papers before she could join her new job.

Initially, Laila was worried about sending her all alone to another state. She could not hold back any longer. She finally asked Nina, "Are you sure you'll be able to live all by yourself? I know that you've been in and out of hostels for a long time. But this time around, you are going to a different state. I'll accompany you for the initial week. Later, you'll have to manage alone."

Nina's confidence was unmatched; she was able to assure Laila that everything would be fine. Laila took Ron's help in making arrangements for Nina's transition. Ron had a big social circle and luckily his friends in Hyderabad did the needful. They searched for a one-room apartment near the hospital. They got the paperwork done and Laila took on the responsibility of ensuring that Nina had a smooth transition.

She requested Sarita to come to Mrs Samson's house for a week so that she could help Nina settle down in the new place. Sarita agreed and brought Harsh along as his summer break was on.

With two big suitcases and two small ones, they boarded the train to their destination. The women were so tired from all the efforts that went into the hurried arrangements and the last-minute packing that they dozed off just half an hour into the journey. After about an hour, Laila woke up to loud screams amidst chaos. She shouted, "Nina, wake up. There's so much smoke here. Looks like there's been a fire!"

Both ran towards the exit along with the other passengers. When they exited, they saw a cloud of smoke emanating from the fire-engulfed coach adjacent to theirs. They heard people crying and calling out for help. Nina told Laila, "Go away from the train and take shelter at a safe distance."

"No, you also come along."

"People need my help here. I can give first aid to the injured. Please leave with the other ladies. Else, you'll get hurt. The fire is getting ferocious. Move…"

Laila refused to go and started assisting the injured passengers along with Nina and the others. Being a nurse, Nina went around fearlessly helping the passengers; Laila supported her. Ambulances arrived and so did the fire tenders. The surroundings were echoing with sirens and screams. The firefighters were evacuating passengers from the coaches. Kids were being carried in blankets. It was a scary scene but Laila and Nina tirelessly did their best.

After a few hours, all that was left was the smell of smoke, remains from the burnt luggage, blood stains everywhere, scattered footwear…each article telling a terrifying story. The scene would have shaken anyone to the core.

After the chaos ended, Laila and Nina got hold of their luggage as their coach had been spared the damage from the fire. Then, they called home to inform everyone that they were safe. Thankfully, Mrs Samson hadn't seen the news since morning. Otherwise, it would have been traumatic for her!

Ron, however, got to know of the incident when the news broke across the country. He was quite stressed and tried to find the whereabouts of Laila and Nina without much success. Although he learned through his sources that their coach was spared the damage, he wanted to hear from Laila. When she saw his missed calls, she called back and he heaved a sigh of relief.

Nina called the hospital's human resource department. Informing them about the situation, she sought a week's time before joining duty. They agreed and hence both of them travelled back to Delhi.

Accidents, disasters, catastrophes,
All echo with screams and tears.
When fellow humans call for help,
Only cooperation can allay their fears.

14

Buddy's Absence

A week later, Nina and Laila reached Hyderabad. Laila took on the responsibility of setting up the house while Nina joined the hospital. She stocked up on vegetables and other grocery items and got the television, microwave and fridge installed. To ensure that Nina didn't have to spend time on household work once she returned to Delhi, Laila paid attention to the minutest of details.

After a hectic week, Laila flew back to Delhi. Ron had booked a flight ticket for her as a surprise gift. Laila was hesitant to accept it but conceded when he said that he just wanted to make up for his absence. He sincerely wished to share her responsibilities. A nervous Laila boarded her first-ever flight. She was constantly in touch with Ron through messages. Once en route, she thought to herself, "What good have I done that Ron does so much for me? Today, as always, he has given me wings."

His comforting gestures always spoke of Laila's importance in his life. It was as if there was an unseen, intangible, subtle thread that bound them. And it certainly held the fibres of unconditional care together. Even as time passed by, the beautiful balance of no expectations from either side intensified their togetherness.

Nina got busy with her job. Back in Delhi, Laila had started noticing changes in Buddy's eating habits. He did not eat on time; sometimes, he ate very little, and at other times, he would throw up after eating. She eventually took him to a veterinarian for a check-up. The doctor prescribed some medicines which were given to Buddy for a week, but no improvement was seen. He was becoming lethargic and frail day by day. She followed up with the doctor who prescribed some tests to be done at a veterinary hospital. The investigation, unfortunately, pointed to an impending organ failure.

Laila, very gradually, broke the news to Mrs Samson. She also told Nina about it. Nina got extremely disturbed and thought of visiting Buddy in Delhi right away.

Some medicines were administered to slow down the progression of the condition and regular monitoring was advised by the doctor. The lively Samson household became morbid. Brown also sensed that something was wrong with his pal. Although Brown used to stroll around on the lawn, Buddy's activity had reduced and he stuck to his doghouse most of the time.

Mrs Samson began to feel low, but Laila would cheer her up by sitting by her side with Buddy on her lap. She used to feed Buddy light food and pamper him with new balls and toys.

Laila and Raju, on Mrs Samson's insistence, would take both canines for evening rides in the car, every now and then. Grooming sessions were regularly done as was the case in good times so that Buddy felt better. Mrs Samson used to get pictures clicked with Buddy as he never shied away from looking into the camera. He could stare and pose for hours together if allowed to do so.

One night, unfortunately, Buddy passed away in his sleep. He had eaten a light meal and slept, but didn't wake up the next day. It was tough for everyone to bid goodbye to the dearly loved member of the Samson household. A silence, a gloominess permeated the atmosphere in the house. Buddy had been like a baby to Mrs Samson and Laila. Despite Laila's best efforts to help her minimize the despair, Mrs Samson's health deteriorated for a brief period afterwards.

To normalize the environment at home, Nina took a week off from work and came home. She spent quality time with Mrs Samson and encouraged her to eat well so that she could regain her health. The most deeply affected member, though, was Brown. The poor chap was left alone; his brother was no longer there to share his doghouse, his meals, his toys and more importantly, every moment of his life. He would sit on the lawn for hours as if waiting for Buddy to come and play with him.

After about six months, things returned to normal and the mood in the house changed as everyone tried their best to adjust to Buddy's physical absence. He had a permanent place in everyone's heart.

One day, Laila and Mrs Samson were chatting on the lawn when the bell rang. When Laila opened the gate, two girls greeted her and gave the reference of Mrs Samson's friend. Actually, they were new in the city and had recently been posted to the Delhi-based branch of their bank. They were introduced to Mrs Samson's friend when they had gone to her house to provide doorstep banking services. On mentioning that they were in dire need of safe accommodation on rent for a month before they were allotted rooms in the residential complex of their bank, Mrs Samson's friend referred them to her. Since there were a couple of vacant rooms in the house, she figured Mrs Samson would be able to help the young girls.

Mrs Samson listened to them patiently, thought about it for a while, and confirmed it over a phone call with her friend. She then allowed them to stay on the first floor. "None of my children have any plans to visit in the coming months. I can help these girls," she thought to herself.

One of the girls asked about the rent. Mrs Samson replied, "Look, you are like my children. I don't have any huge requirements. You can stay here for a month as a family member. Just make sure that you don't mess up my house."

"Aunty, be assured, we will not disappoint you. We just need a secure place to stay and your house meets our requirements. Please let us know the rent so we can proceed further."

"I don't think you girls have understood what I just said." The girls seemed confused.

Mrs Samson smiled at Laila and asked, "Laila, did I ask for rent?"

A confident Laila replied, "Yes! A promise to keep the room as it is and no mess in the kitchen – that's the only rent!"

The girls were on cloud nine. They had neither expected nor experienced such good fortune before. The next day, the girls moved in with their rucksacks and trolley bags. Laila showed them their room on the first floor. They kept their belongings and went to work, as they had to report early.

Anyone and everyone who had ever got a chance to stay at Mrs Samson's house enjoyed the warmth and love that the home had to offer. The two girls weren't an exception either. Within a span of three to four days, they became a part of the family. They tried to convince Mrs Samson a couple of times to accept rent from them but the old lady refused.

Mrs Samson hadn't just given them a place to live, instead, she gave them a home away from home. They felt indebted to her, so they made a pact with Laila: They offered to cook special lunch on weekends for all four of them. The four weeks of their stay were full of laughter, south-Indian food and lively chats.

Time flew by and they moved into their rooms at the residential complex of the bank. However, they left the house, promising to visit whenever they had some free time.

Transience is the word to characterise
The essence of this life;
As one moment moulds into the next,
Adaptation is what we can do best.

15

Mrs Samson's Health Issues

After about a month, Irene visited Mrs Samson for a week. She was on an official trip but managed to spend as much time as possible with her. She was the most loved member of Mrs Samson's family. A pleasant and poised person, she got along equally well with both the elders and the younger lot. Her parents also lived in Delhi, and they made it a point to visit Mrs Samson every couple of months.

Interestingly, whenever Irene visited, Mrs Samson would tell her to get lipsticks and perfumes for her which she would gift to her friends. Irene was always happy to oblige. On a sultry afternoon, when Irene was sitting by her side, Mrs Samson said to her, "I've been asking you all these years to get me these gifts…don't you ever feel burdened?"

"Don't embarrass me, Mom. This is such a small thing. We live so far away. Instead, we should be here, taking care of you and fulfilling all your wishes."

"Darling, your emotions and upbringing keep you attached to me. It is more than enough that you acknowledge your responsibility. I'm glad you are so different from Donna. You know what, when Eric and Donna visited India for the first time after their wedding, Donna wanted to bring me a gift. I told her I would be happy to accept whatever she brought me, but she pestered me to tell her about my likes and dislikes."

Irene interrupted, "Really Mom! That sounds so unlike Donna."

"Absolutely! I told her to bring me a cotton sweater in any pastel shade. She brought me a baby pink one."

"Oh, did she?"

"Yes, but it had these oranges, bananas and apples printed all over. I thought, maybe she searched for it in a kids' store!"

Irene was amused as she said, "Oh Mom, you are so frank! If Donna hears this, she'll be mad and Eric will have to bear the brunt of it."

Mrs Samson took Irene's hand and kissed it. "Why should I bother? I feel blessed that I have you, my dear," she said, sliding a gold ring on her daughter-in-law's finger.

Irene was surprised and she loved it. The ring had her initials on it. She hugged and thanked Mrs Samson for the beautiful gift.

A week full of pampering flew by like an aeroplane at jet speed. They went out for lunch a couple of times. She took Mrs Samson to her favourite outlets to shop for clothes. They visited a few religious places and then she flew back home.

A couple of days later, Mrs Samson complained of uneasiness and chest pain one morning. Laila wanted to believe that it was just anxiety, but she thought it would be better if Mrs Samson saw a doctor. She took her to the hospital and her echocardiogram came out abnormal. She informed Irene immediately. Since Irene was from an allied medical field, she knew several doctors here and abroad. She then reached out to her contacts who arranged for an appointment with a cardiologist at one of the super speciality hospitals. There, all the tests were done and it was ascertained that Mrs Samson had had a mild cardiac event. Fortunately, her parameters were stable and a medical procedure was advised to avoid any such incidents in the future.

A couple of days later, Eric arrived to be with his mother. She was then admitted to the hospital, and after successful and uneventful treatment, she was discharged. A day before her son was to leave, Mrs Samson developed a severe breathing problem. She had to be rushed to the hospital again and she was administered treatment to relieve her symptoms. Later, they returned home.

Laila thought to herself, "This year is turning out to be a tough one for Mrs Samson. First, Buddy left us. Even before she could recover from this loss, she developed cardiac issues and additional health problems. However, there is no denying that her sedentary lifestyle has contributed to her ill health. Her advancing age is introducing a barrage of health issues."

Disturbed by her frail health, Mrs Samson's younger son, Roger, also planned a visit immediately. He arrived after a fortnight to stay with her for a month. He had always been the apple of her eye. When he came, she began showing some improvement on an emotional level. It was as if she had started to regain her stability.

One day, while Laila was talking to Ron over the phone, she said, "You know, Roger eats all his meals with her and sits with her on the lawn for hours every day in a bid to sincerely listen to her unexpressed emotions. He knows that she feels lonely despite having people around her. He has taken up the responsibility of reviving her jovial nature which has vanished into thin air. Roger acknowledges that his mother is a strong lady, but she needs her children to hold her hand in these weak moments."

"It's his upbringing, thanks to Mrs Samson's efforts, that's shining through," Ron said.

One day, Mrs Samson held her son's hand tightly and said, "You've been here for long. Now, you should go back to your family. They are your responsibility. I'm better now. Don't worry, I will be fine."

He put his arms around her and kissed her hand. With tears in his eyes, he said, "Mom, you are our priority. You've shocked us with your health issues. We aren't as strong as you! I'm glad that you are getting better. I'll stay with you for some more time, and then I'll head back home. Irene seems to be managing everything well over there." He put his head on her lap for some time while she patted him as if putting a small child to sleep.

A week later, he left, and by then, Mrs Samson's health had improved considerably.

One morning, Laila was watering the plants on the lawn when a courier delivery vehicle arrived outside their gate. The delivery boy rang the bell and Laila opened the gate. Mrs Samson was also watching from the living room as the door was ajar. A huge parcel had arrived. "A parcel for Mrs Samson," said the delivery boy. From the size of the carton, it looked like a refrigerator.

Laila asked the delivery boy, "Where is this from?"

"Madam, I don't know who the sender is, but it was ordered in Hyderabad."

As soon as she heard this, she guessed it was from Nina. She signed the receipt and the delivery boy left it in the veranda. She called Raju to assist her in opening it. The package had red and pink ribbons tied around it. They cut open the carton carefully. It was a beautiful, robust, wooden, rocking chair all covered up in bubble wrap.

A note on the package read, "My dear DG, I hope you like this chair. I've been saving money for this ever since your previous one broke. I hope you enjoy your time on the lawn, sitting in this chair. Stay well. Love, Nina."

Laila gave the note to Mrs Samson along with her spectacles. Mrs Samson teared up when she read it and hugged Laila. "Such a caring child she is! I'm so lucky to have both of you in my life," she said, as she went towards the chair and sat in it.

Laila clicked a picture of Mrs Samson in the chair and sent it to Nina. Then, they talked on the phone. "My child, you didn't have to do this!" said Mrs Samson and then profusely thanked her and showered her with blessings. A sheen of pride was seen in Laila's eyes. She was seeing the fruits of the virtues that she had instilled in Nina while she was growing up.

Later in the evening, Mrs Samson rang up her kids and joyously told them about the gift from Nina. She was very happy and so was everyone else except Donna. Donna seemed indifferent. However, Mrs Samson made it a point to show the chair to her. The old lady wanted to tell her that she had found a loving family member in every person who was associated with her. Maybe, she wished that Donna would change her attitude someday.

Seniority is synonymous with abundance
Of experiences and emotional maturity.
All that lives can then be enriched with
Is love, care and concern in absolute purity.

16

A New Beginning for Laila

One evening, when Laila was out on a walk, she met her friend Raashi. Raashi was the housekeeper of Mrs Samson's friend. They used to meet when the old ladies got together for tea and games once a month. While chatting casually about daily life, Raashi confided in Laila. "My son is finding mathematics tough. His scores are low and his teacher asked me to pay more attention to his studies. He is in seventh grade. Do you know anyone who can help? I'm not educated myself and I won't be able to pay the hefty fees for private tutors."

"Well, don't worry, I may be able to solve your problem. I've helped Nina with the subject all through her schooling." Laila told her to bring her son's mathematics book the next day so that she could have a look.

A few weeks later, Laila began devoting an hour every day to helping the child with his studies. Six months down the line, he showed marked improvement, and Raashi expressed her gratitude to Laila for her help. The word spread fast. Soon, Laila's evenings were spent guiding a bunch of kids with their homework. All of it was voluntary service for those who couldn't afford tutors. Mrs Samson was happy to see Laila getting busy with something other than household chores and she encouraged her to continue her good work.

One day, when Ron was visiting, as he did so once every six months, he told Laila, "Think about getting a graduate degree through a correspondence course. Perhaps you could even do a teacher's training course over time." He could see Laila's confidence grow by leaps and bounds.

"I think you are right. I like your idea. Presently, I can comfortably spare two to three hours a day for such activities."

Mrs Samson also motivated her to do the same. Soon, with Mrs Lalitha's help, she enrolled in a correspondence course. It was a three-year-long course and by the end of it, she would have a graduate degree.

Laila was dedicated and meticulous in her work. Right from the beginning, she set aside two hours for study and another couple of hours for teaching underprivileged kids. Since Laila was returning to her studies after a considerable gap, she occasionally faced troubles. However, Ron helped her stay focused. He would calm her down over phone calls and motivate her whenever needed.

One day, Laila had to travel all the way to Central Delhi to purchase some books. Darya Ganj in Central Delhi is a major hub for books, both educational and literary. Laila was travelling by bus and had to change buses twice to get to her destination. For the first time, she was covering a remarkable distance in Delhi and that too by public transport. It was an ordeal for her.

First, she got on the wrong connecting bus. Then, she had to find her way through packed buses to disembark at the right stop. When she was in the middle of the market, she got a call from Ron. She could barely hear him. "Laila, don't forget to go to the famous eatery I told you about.

Get Jalebi for yourself and take some back for Mrs Samson too," he said.

"I feel lost here and you are talking about Jalebis!"

Ron couldn't stop laughing.

"Laila, relax! This friend of mine who told me about the Jalebis, also said that Central Delhi is vastly different from where you live. Take it easy. It is a different experience. Enjoy it."

"Mrs Samson insisted on bringing Raju along. I should have listened to her. At least, he could have guided me through these tortuous lanes."

"I just remembered, you must try the chaat there, Laila!"

"Ron, Stop it!"

Ron had some urgent work so they ended the conversation. Laila continued with her shopping and returned home later that evening.

Six months into the course, Laila was about to write her semester exams when Nina fell terribly ill. Laila was in a fix; she wanted to help Nina which meant that she would miss her exams. Her motherly instincts overrode the possibility of a practical solution. Acknowledging the importance of Laila's exams, Nina told her not to come. Initially, Laila didn't agree to it. Later, it was decided that Nina would get admitted in the hospital so that she could get the required care. Once Laila finished with her exams, she would go to take care of Nina. This suggestion was actually Ron's!

Nina considered Ron as part of the family, and she often took his help when she needed to convince her elder sister about something. He offered genuine, practical solutions.

Laila, being sensitive, always gave more importance to her heart rather than her head, while Nina was more of a practical and objective thinker when it came to handling complex situations. Perhaps she had developed this quality due to her profession, which required swift and justifiable judgement.

A month later, Nina recovered from typhoid, and Laila, having finished her exams, went to see her. Ron had been promoted to the rank of a Captain in the Army and was visiting Hyderabad on temporary duty so they planned the visit accordingly. He spent an evening with them and they all had dinner together. Ron treated them at a fine eatery. He then headed back, while Laila stayed on for one week.

Back in Delhi, Raashi was taking care of Mrs Samson. Actually, Sarita, who used to fill in for Laila, had developed arthritis, and so she was not in good health. Raashi was largely free for a month, as the lady whom she worked for had gone abroad to spend some time with her daughter. Thus, Laila requested Raashi to fill in for her. Raashi was more than happy to help Laila out, as she had helped her son with his studies. Later, Laila returned to Delhi and got engrossed in her daily routine once again.

A great beginning becomes so
Not just by the journey's culmination,
But by the complete story:
The desires and the compulsions.

17

That Scary Month

Miles away, Mrs Samson's grandson was to graduate in a couple of months and her daughter-in-law, Irene, wanted her to be present for the occasion. At first, Mrs Samson refused due to her age and ill-health, but for Irene's sake, she agreed eventually.

To ensure that the old lady felt comfortable on the long flight, Irene came all the way to Delhi to accompany Mrs Samson. Their relationship was different and deep. It was going to be a month-long trip and Mrs Samson planned to stay with her elder son also for a week.

Mrs Samson used to video call Laila every day and they would chat for a good half-hour discussing how they spent their day. One evening, Mrs Samson told her, "Laila, I'm leaving for Eric's place today itself because he has some work commitments in the coming weeks."

"Okay, Madam, but do take your medicines along. All four organisers are filled. The blue one has extra medicines in it."

"Yes, I'll be carrying one organiser. I'll be there for a week. Irene has already packed my stuff and she has put it in my bag."

"And remember to take your lung exerciser and inhaler with you."

"Yes, it's snowing at Eric's place. It will be cold. Although temperatures inside are controlled, I may need them."

Laila was very cautious about Mrs Samson's health and therefore, most of their daily talks were invariably centred around her medicines and wellbeing.

One day, when Laila was taking Brown for a walk in the locality, she noticed two young boys standing outside the house. She got suspicious because they were attempting to peep through the half-open gate. They were dressed in ragged clothing, carried overstuffed rucksacks and looked scary. Raju was washing the car parked at the sidewall of the house. He had left the gate half-open while carrying a bucket of water outside. He was unaware of the movements of the boys.

Laila sprang into action. She steered Brown towards the gate. The canine sniffed that something was not right, so he started barking. Seeing this, the boys vanished.

When Laila discussed this incident with Ron at night, he advised, "Be cautious and have Brown sleep in your room. Double lock the gate from the inside."

"I will be cautious. Don't keep your phone on silent mode at night. I might call you if I feel the need. Security guards will be on duty anyway at night."

"Don't worry! The area is relatively safe. Do keep the pepper spray handy. You'll be fine. Good night and take care."

"Good night, Ron."

Thankfully, the night was uneventful and Laila woke up to the milkman's call. Raju had already arrived early morning on Laila's request and was at the park adjacent to the block. Then, he took the car for refuelling and later accompanied Sarita to her doctor's appointment. During the day, Laila felt a bit uneasy because of the fear over what had happened the previous evening. She called her friend Raashi to spend an hour with her. After Raashi left, she tried to keep herself busy with some books.

As the afternoon rolled into the evening, she started getting anxious. When she talked to Mrs Samson that day, she didn't mention anything about it although the old lady remarked that she didn't sound normal. Mrs Samson went on to tell her that she had had a wonderful time at her grandson's graduation party. "It was organised at a posh banquet hall. I met his batchmates; they were so courteous. A couple of his friends sat with me all through the evening and talked in their unique accents. I thoroughly enjoyed myself," she said.

"Oh, that's so sweet."

"One of them was from Europe and he invited me to visit him if I planned a trip to the continent. He showed me pictures of his family on his phone. One of his classmates even brought a home-baked pudding for me. She was Mexican, and it was her granny's recipe!"

"Children have the purest of hearts, Madam."

"Yes, and a few of Irene's and Roger's friends who are choir vocalists gave a special performance in my honour. It was a heartening gesture! It has been a refreshing trip so far."

"I'm so happy for you, Madam." A few minutes later, the conversation ended leaving a jolly feeling in Laila's mind although temporary.

Later, when she talked to Nina, she couldn't hide her anxiety but refrained from talking about it. Nina called Ron to inform him about it. Ron pacified her saying,

"Had there been anything to tell, Laila would have told me. Don't worry, I'll check with her once again."

Since Raashi knew about the situation, she talked about it with her employer, Mrs Gupta, who was Mrs Samson's close friend. "Either you spend the night at Mrs Samson's house or have Laila over for the night. She shouldn't stay there alone," she suggested.

"Madam, I'll just talk to Laila," Raashi said.

Meanwhile, Mrs Gupta also informed the Resident Welfare Association about the issue.

It was decided that Raashi would spend the night at Mrs Samson's house. Laila was accompanied by Brown too. According to her, it wouldn't have been proper to take Brown to someone's house.

The next day, Laila explained the situation to Mrs Samson who then requested her friend to let Raashi stay with Laila at night till she returned home a week later. Ron went out of his way to visit Laila once during this time, just for a few hours, to ensure her wellbeing.

A day later, there was a theft in the neighbourhood. Thankfully, as everyone was alert, the two boys were nabbed before they could escape. This automatically brought down Laila's anxiety levels.

Mrs Samson also returned after a while. Finally, Laila, Nina, and Ron heaved a sigh of relief.

Caution is the shield
That'll protect you all along.
Mostly, it's your only armour,
And it is undoubtedly strong.

18

Here Comes Turmoil

A couple of years passed by, and Laila completed her graduation. Nina got promoted and signed up for a special course to be trained as an emergency nurse. Raju's son, Harsh, was turning out to be a brilliant student and aspired to become a doctor. All the youngsters were climbing the ladder of success, and Mrs Samson accepted the quirks of advancing age with grace!

Sarita's health took a downward turn due to arthritis. Everyone was concerned as they were a big family tied together not by blood but by the heart.

Nina was in Delhi for a week as a part of her training at a premier institute. It was springtime and the lawn was full of healthy, colourful flowers. Mrs Samson was seated in her rocking chair. Nina was enjoying her walk barefooted on the green grass; Brown sat by Mrs Samson's side, while Laila was preparing lunch. Suddenly, Brown started barking incessantly. Nina turned around to calm him down and got the shock of her life. Mrs Samson had fallen unconscious. Her upper body was leaning over the right arm of the chair and Brown was licking her hand.

Nina rushed towards her and tried to bring her back to her senses. She checked her heartbeat and found a very weak pulse. She shouted for help. Laila and Raju rushed to the garden and the trio tried their best to revive her by sprinkling water and patting her. When nothing seemed to work, Nina being a trained nurse, began giving CPR to Mrs Samson. Within moments, she was able to revive Mrs Samson's pulse. She called for an ambulance and Mrs Samson was taken to the nearest hospital. Laila and Raju followed by a car while Nina accompanied Mrs Samson in the ambulance.

After a two-day stay at the hospital, during which some special tests were conducted and a remedial procedure was done, Mrs Samson was brought home. Nina stayed home for another couple of days, so she shared Laila's responsibilities in the evening and at night-time when she wasn't on duty. Eventually, the situation settled and things returned to normal. Instrumental in administering timely care to her DG, Nina had saved her. Undoubtedly, her presence was reassuring enough for the old lady to recover fast.

One day, Rita, Ron's sister, told Laila over a phone call that she wanted to meet her.

"Yes, sure. Are you heading somewhere on vacation?"

"No, I'll be travelling straight to Delhi and back. Just wanted to meet you to discuss something important with you."

Laila agreed and Rita came to Delhi for a very brief period. The issue concerned Laila and Ron. Laila did have some idea about what it was, as Ron had already told her that his family was insisting that he get married. When the women met, Rita asked Laila about her and Ron's equation upfront. She wanted to know Laila's viewpoint regarding marriage.

Laila and Ron were clear that marriage was not a viable option, as Laila had responsibilities towards Nina and

Mrs Samson; she couldn't leave the old lady alone at this stage in her life. She conveyed the same to Rita, and the conversation ended on a sombre note despite Rita's best efforts to convince Laila about giving it another thought. A disappointed Rita shared the developments with her parents.

Prior to that, Ron had also conveyed to Rita about Laila's position but she wanted to make an effort nevertheless. Ron wasn't in favour of her talking to Laila about the issue but she went ahead anyway.

That night, Ron called Laila, but she didn't take his call. A sensitive girl, Laila wanted Ron to choose a suitable partner for himself as she didn't want him to keep waiting for her all his life. She was angry at him for not paying attention to himself. Simultaneously, she was upset about her predicament. She simply sent him a message which read, "Will talk tomorrow." Ron understood her emotions very well, so he gave her the required time and space.

When they talked the next day, a heated argument ensued. Laila tried relentlessly to convince him to move ahead in life, but Ron wasn't ready to give in. Consequently, Laila refrained from talking to him for the next two days.

Such grave developments didn't escape Mrs Samson's eyes. She was concerned and asked Laila, "What is the matter? Why aren't you taking Ron's calls? You've never behaved like this before!" Laila dodged the questions and got busy with her daily chores.

After two days, Ron and Laila discussed the matter again, and post an hour-long talk, Laila was able to convince Ron to move on in life!

She was unaware if this was a win or loss for her. Evidently, Ron hadn't agreed wholeheartedly. On the other hand, when Ron gave in, Laila felt a void for the first time. They were inseparable. Sadly enough, she was unable to realize this.

One night, she became very uneasy and said to herself, "This is such a terrible feeling. It's as if my heart is sinking and I will run out of breath. I've never felt like this before." After all, there was no denying that she had a surreal attachment to Ron. However, in the following weeks, they seldom talked, and the distance which had never mattered before started turning into a deep gorge between the duo.

Laila felt low over the thought of letting go of the precious bond she had with Ron, but she was doing it for his sake…at least that's what she thought.

Ron's family, without wasting any time, arranged a meeting with a prospective bride, Shivani. They informed Ron about it and told him to come to Dehradun to meet her. Ron tried to put off the meeting for a couple of months but had to finally give in to his family's repeated requests. He went home and they met.

Being an honest man, during their very first meeting, he explained his situation to Shivani, who was compassionate enough to allow him some more time to decide on whether he was interested in the alliance or not. "Please agree to this relationship only if you can give your 100% to the marriage. Give it some thought, till then, I'll wait. You can let me know about your decision in a week's time," Shivani told him. Her words made Ron extremely uncomfortable and guilty. He realized that he had to be ready for marriage by choice and not under pressure.

He mustered enough courage and told his parents about it. "I won't be able to decide on marriage anytime soon. You need to give me some more time," he told them.

His mother, like any other parent, was eager to see him as a married man. She said, "She is a perfect match for you. She is well educated, good-natured and we've known her family for years. What are you waiting for?"

"Mummy, if you want me to be happy, you must let me decide."

His mother became irritated and seeing this, his father had to intervene. "Can both of you take it easy?" he said.

"I've been wanting him to get married for so long. Don't I have any right over him? I am growing old. I want to play with my grandkids. He doesn't listen at all!" his mother said. The conversation ended on this note.

A couple of days later, Ron made a courtesy call and thanked Shivani for her patience and understanding. "May you be blessed with an equally mature and understanding partner as you are," he said, as he bid her goodbye.

**The intensity of pain, which by nature, is emotional,
Can be gauged only by the actions of the affected soul.**

19

The Mishmash of Emotions

Ron re-joined duty and after about a month, he decided to talk to Laila. She was still coping with the high and low tides of emotions that drenched her every now and then. She took his call and plainly said, "Hi, umm…how have you been?"

"Hi Laila, I'm doing fine. How are you?"

"I'm good. So, what have you decided? Are you going to marry the girl whom you met?"

"Listen, I can't sail in two boats. Whether anyone agrees with me or not, I must be clear before I take the plunge."

"Fair enough, Ron. As long as you keep your options open, it's okay."

Laila had lost her chirpiness, and Ron sounded equally drained as he explained the situation to her. In a dilemma, she was unable to understand her feelings. She secretly felt secure knowing that Ron hadn't moved on. But she was also guilty on some level, as she couldn't give Ron the gift of their togetherness. She knew, he totally deserved it. However, her circumstances wouldn't allow her to do so. That day, for the first time, she accepted that Ron held a significant place in her heart and life.

Although she felt this way, she held back her feelings and tears and told Ron, "Maybe you really need more time to free up some space in your heart and mind before you decide on a suitable partner for yourself."

An irked Ron replied, "Don't you think everyone is being harsh with me? Parents have their own expectations; you have your limitations and I totally respect all of it. What am I asking for? Just that I get my share of peace. I am the only one without any expectations from anyone!"

Laila broke down that very moment and said, "I'm sorry Ron, I'm so sorry!" They took some time to regain their composure as the silence spread like a blanket, putting an end to this contentious discussion.

The next six months were even tougher for both of them. They talked less frequently and rarely met, each fighting their own emotional battles.

After a while, Ron was posted to a different station in the southern part of the country. Before he made the move, he asked Laila if they could meet. She stood firmly by her decision and with a heavy heart, declined. Ron accepted her decision.

Stress had taken its toll on the duo, and as a result, Laila's health took a downward turn. She developed hypertension and related issues. Nina became worried and came to stay with her for a week. Down in the south, Rita visited Ron, as she knew that he was struggling too. But nothing worked!

Rita felt that if the situation was to be saved from getting worse, Ron had to be given his independence. She went to the village for a week, hoping to convince their parents. Her mother insisted on meeting Ron, but Rita somehow managed to dissuade her from doing so.

A year passed by, and Nina completed her training and joined a private hospital as an emergency nurse. Her working hours increased and so did the pressures related to her job. She was not able to connect as much with Laila as she wanted to, but she tried her best to keep in touch through texts during the day.

Back in Delhi, Laila tried to keep herself busy round-the-clock. Sometimes, she would spend extra hours with the kids who needed help with their studies. At other times, she volunteered with gardening at the local park. Mrs Samson, of course, got the major chunk of Laila's time. However, the young woman was in a state where she didn't want to remain idle for long periods. This meant that she was on the verge of a burnout.

Nina was so far away that she wasn't able to assess the situation very well. Laila only confided in her friend, Raashi. Over the past few months, they had become the best of friends. Raashi, however, was of the view that Laila and Ron were punishing themselves unnecessarily. She made sure that Laila took care of her health and she kept an eye on Ron too. One day, she attempted to convince Laila to call Ron and ask about his wellbeing. "For a while, stop controlling the way you want Ron's life to be. He deserves to be cared for; he deserves to be understood. He's been a part of your life for so long. You are not being fair to him."

Laila called and spoke to Ron. Their discussion turned out to be a breather for both of them. In the following months, they started talking more often. Rita saw a marked improvement in Ron's state of mind. Her view about Ron's and Laila's interdependence became firm and this was when Ron first got his sister's unwavering support.

Six months later, Rita informed Laila that Ron was sick from a liver ailment and had been admitted to the hospital for emergency surgery. "My husband and I are going to look him up. If you feel comfortable, we can take you along. Your presence will definitely uplift his spirit," Rita said.

Laila readily agreed and went with them. By the time they reached the hospital, the surgery had been done and he was to be discharged the following day. Only Rita and her husband met him at the hospital, and when he was discharged, Laila surprised him at his residence. Tears, smiles, and a warm embrace defined the moment. Laila had planned to stay till the evening after which she was to board the return flight to Delhi. Her gesture and presence were enough to clear the air between her and Ron. They were not lovers and there wasn't any scope for such a development in the near future, but they were definitely dedicated partners.

After a week, Rita also returned home when Ron's health improved and he re-joined duty. After this bout of illness, Laila started talking to him regularly and they revived their connect.

Heartache is very different
From the pain of letting go;
The void from the latter
Is permanent, you know!

20

Mixed Bag

Laila and Nina were half-sisters, but time and circumstances had forced Laila to take up the role of a mother to Nina. With so many years going into Nina's upbringing, Laila could easily read most of Nina's unexpressed emotions. During Nina's last visit home, Laila noticed that she was spending a considerable amount of time on late-night phone calls. She looked happier than usual, used loads of perfume, seemed slightly over-conscious of her appearance, and talked in a more mature manner.

Laila didn't feel it was right to probe her at this point in time. After some time passed by, she casually asked her over a phone call about her future plans and marriage. Nina opened up to her about Ravi, her love-interest, who was from the same profession. They had become good friends just six months after she had joined her present job. Laila also enquired about his family and was happy to hear about the new development in Nina's life. She excitedly said, "This means, we'll have a lot to talk about the next time you come home, or maybe we'll get to meet your special one soon!" Nina blushed and giggled.

Giving her some motherly advice, Laila said, "I hope you've taken time before deciding to turn the friendship into a life-long relationship." Nina, being a mature and independent girl, took her sister's advice in the right spirit.

The next day, Laila broke the news to Ron. He was very excited and joyous. A responsible young man, he spontaneously said, "You don't worry, I'll get his background checked."

Laila laughed at his reaction and said, "Of course, Mr Protective, but first Nina has to be sure."

"Yes, yes, Madam!"

The next morning, Laila talked about the matter with Mrs Samson. The old lady was ecstatic. She instructed Laila, "Call Nina right away, I want to talk to her."

"Madam, she's at work now. I'll connect you to her in the evening."

"Okay, sit here and tell me more about Ravi."

The old lady's grandmotherly instincts were at their peak. She didn't let go off Laila's hand until she repeated each and every detail. Later, she told her to prepare chocolate-walnut muffins because she wanted to celebrate.

In the evening, they video-called Nina and Mrs Samson had a long chat with her. She asked so many details that Laila had to politely interrupt the call, as Nina had become conscious and nervous too. She wanted both of them to remain excited and happy. Grandparents have their own way of showing concern and affection, which sometimes gets overwhelming for youngsters. Laila's maturity and understanding were amply evident in the way she conducted her life.

That night, when Ron dialled Laila, he seemed a bit under the weather. "I'm feeling unwell. Since afternoon, I've developed pain in the lower abdomen."

"Did you eat spicy food?" Laila asked.

"No, I had simple lunch and this pain is different. I've never experienced it before. It's a pinching pain. I took over-the-counter pain medication and am hoping for it to set things right."

"Ron, you must alert your friends so that they can help you if need be. I'll keep checking on you over the phone though."

The next morning, when Laila called, he complained of fever and vomiting. She told him to see a doctor immediately. He went to the MI room, and the doctor prescribed a course of antibiotics. Two days after taking the antibiotics, his condition didn't improve. Laila discussed the matter with Nina, who suggested that he follow up with the doctor without delay. By the time Laila got back to him, he had developed chills, and his friends had arrived to shift him to the emergency room. Laila constantly kept in touch and also informed Rita about the development.

A few hours later, Laila got to know that he had to undergo an emergency appendectomy and had since been shifted to the postoperative room. She informed Rita immediately, who also got a call through the official channel regarding the matter. Rita was expecting a baby, so she could not travel to visit him. Laila offered to go, but Rita and her husband advised her against going alone, as it would be difficult for her to manage things all by herself: Travelling down south and commuting to a remote area would be difficult.

They got to know from Ron's friends that he was doing better. Because it was a minimally invasive surgery, he was to be discharged in two days' time. Ron also called to convey the same.

Laila was stressed thinking about how Ron would be managing. However, things improved fast, and Ron was back on duty in a week. One day, Brown passed away, leaving everyone teary-eyed, including his new friend, Tiny, who had been adopted into the family recently.

Nina decided to visit Laila for a couple of days, as it had been long since they had last met. She wished to spend some quality time with her elder sister. Laila lovingly prepared her favourite food: Pasta in white sauce, spinach ravioli, garlic mushrooms and cold coffee.

As soon as Nina arrived, Mrs Samson hugged her tightly and made her sit next to her. Nina held on to Laila's hand till Mrs Samson let go off hers, just like a small child holding on to its mother's hand. She was nervous and slightly shy as she knew that the old lady's inquisitiveness would lead to a round of rapid-fire questions! A few moments later, Laila told her to go upstairs to change and signalled that she would follow.

She had already kept cold coffee and some munchies for Nina in their room. The girls spent an hour upstairs. Later, all three of them devoured the scrumptious lunch.

Scary, soulful, saddening, soothing or simply alive:
There is music in every phase of life.
Whatever be the mood of the notes,
Peace through adaptability one can surely derive.

21

Not Again!

One evening, Laila was talking to Raashi in the park when the latter mentioned that her younger sister, Sakhi, was going to arrive in Delhi in a couple of days.

"How old is she?" Laila asked.

"She's nineteen."

"You should convince her to study further. She can start working after a couple of years. These days vocational courses are helpful in getting better and higher paying jobs."

"I too wish that she studies further. I send home most part of my earnings. We try to manage here with my husband's salary."

"Hmm…but still things don't work out? I can understand," said Laila.

"Actually, my family is finding it difficult to make ends meet. We have two younger brothers too. There isn't much scope for earning in the village, so my family has decided to send Sakhi here for work. I am also on the lookout, but I request that you keep Sakhi in mind if you come across a suitable job opportunity," Raashi said.

When Laila returned home, she remembered that she hadn't watered the plants that evening. She had Tiny settle down in his kennel and proceeded to fetch the water hose and sprinkler from inside.

"I've been calling for you. Where have you been?" Mrs Samson asked her.

"Madam, I messed things up a bit today. By mistake, I took Tiny out for his walk an hour earlier. You were sleeping so I didn't want to disturb you. I'm sorry. Do you need anything?"

"Yes, I want to have some tea, I have a headache."

Laila swiftly prepared ginger-infused tea and served it to her.

Later, during dinner, she told Mrs Samson about Raashi's sister, Sakhi, as many of the old lady's friends had caretakers and the need for substitutes often arose when any of them took leave. Moreover, Mrs Samson was of helping nature and Laila thought that she'd try her best to place Sakhi as a house help in a home within her friends' circle.

Back in Dehradun, Rita gave birth to twin boys. Ron broke the news to Laila that very evening. Both were thrilled and congratulated Rita and her family. Six months later, both planned a trip to their village in Dehradun to meet Rita who was visiting after her delivery.

Mrs Samson had employed Sakhi temporarily to share Laila's housekeeping duties. Not that Laila was overworked, but the old lady wanted to help Sakhi, as the poor girl was jobless even three months after arriving in Delhi. She was good at her work, and Laila mentored her well. When Laila went to Dehradun to visit Rita, Sakhi took charge of the house.

Two cute little boys, one in Laila's arms and the other with Ron. What a relief it was for Rita! At last, she got some time to relax. Ron's mother said to him in sheer angst, "Had you got married, you would have been a father by now." Ron's parents had never totally given up on coaxing him into marriage.

Rita whispered to her mother, "You are not being fair, Mummy. Ron's visiting after so long, and Laila is also with us. Why are you making things awkward for them?" Without waiting for a response, she got up and took Laila into the other room. An uneasy Laila felt the pinch but didn't know how to react, so she just let it pass.

An argument ensued between Ron and his mother. "We, as parents, are concerned that once you cross the suitable age for marriage, it will be very difficult to find a bride for you," his mother said. Perhaps his father too thought that Ron was not acting mature. But he was too liberal a father to force his idea on Ron. His mother continued, "Today, you are refusing to get married, but as the years pass by, you'll start feeling lonely. Friendship cannot replace the companionship that comes with marriage. What if Laila finds a partner someday and severs her friendly ties with you?"

Ron angrily replied, "Please don't drag Laila into this. It's my decision, and our friendship is unconditional."

Ron's father intervened and told the duo to calm down saying, "Speak softly, both of you, or we can discuss this later. The mood of the house is being dampened. Rita is also feeling uneasy. Can't you see this?"

Ron's parents weren't happy with his decision but they tried not to hurt Laila. They had known her from childhood and they cared for her. However, obviously, they too didn't agree with Laila's decision to dedicate her life to Mrs Samson. Earlier, they had tried to convince her to get married citing similar reasons they gave to Ron. Maybe they couldn't envision the old lady's role in her life as Laila saw it, or maybe Laila's level of commitment was unimaginable.

Back in Delhi, Mrs Samson's health deteriorated suddenly after she had a fall in the bathroom. Sakhi informed Laila that Mrs Samson had been admitted to the hospital. Laila immediately cut her trip short and boarded the next train to Delhi. When she reached the hospital, she was shocked to see Mrs Samson's state. The old lady had suffered a brain haemorrhage which had left her partially paralysed.

She hugged Mrs Samson and said, "Madam, I've come back. Don't worry." She wiped away Mrs Samson's tears. She informed Mrs Samson's son about the incident. Two days later, he arrived. It was a crucial situation and the old lady had to be operated upon to have the clot removed. Thankfully, the surgery was successful and Mrs Samson showed signs of improvement. Her doctors advised that she would need the assistance of a full-time trained nurse for a few months.

Nina offered to arrange for the nurse through her contacts. Mrs Samson was discharged from the hospital. Three months later, with collective efforts from Laila, a nursing assistant, a compassionate yet strict physiotherapist, a proper diet, and medications, Mrs Samson recovered to a great extent. Although she was able to move about with a walker, Laila made sure that she was by her side 24/7.

Ron also visited Mrs Samson when he was on his way to join duty. She was happy to see him. He brought along a bouquet of roses for her which were her favourite. Thankfully, with time, things returned to normal.

Oftentimes, when we feel bound
By the shackles of unsaid norms,
Life steps up and teaches us
The art of survival in such storms.

22

The Ever-Gracious Mrs Samson

Sakhi was, by then, permanently employed in the Samson household as Laila's assistant. It had more to do with the generous nature of Mrs Samson. The old lady was kind enough to think about everyone around her. She would constantly inquire about the wellbeing of Sarita and Harsh too. For some time now, she was aware that Sarita's arthritis was giving her a tough time.

Out of sheer concern and the inclination to help, one day, Mrs Samson instructed Raju, "Bring Sarita here for some time so that she can be taken care of. During monsoons, her arthritis gets worse. Last year, during this time, she wasn't able to go about her daily household chores even."

"Thank you for thinking about us, Madam. As you know, Harsh has taken a gap-year post his schooling to prepare for his medical entrance exams. When Sarita cannot, he prepares lunch and dinner. He is a very responsible child," Raju said.

Mrs Samson persisted, "I know and I'm happy about it. However, if both of them come here, the child will get some relief and he can spend more time studying."

Laila was also of the same opinion but she didn't intervene. She was very particular about her demeanour in the house. "It's a good idea. But it's totally Mrs Samson's call, and I should refrain from commenting," she thought.

However, Raju and Sarita were sceptical about bothering Mrs Samson with their financial responsibilities. They tried to put off the idea, but how could anyone deny Mrs Samson's request? Finally, on her insistence, Sarita and Harsh moved to Mrs Samson's house. Since Sarita could not climb stairs, Mrs Samson gave her a room on the ground floor.

One day, when Laila was busy teaching kids in the afternoon, she heard a strange noise from the lawn. At first, she ignored it. However, when it didn't stop, she rushed towards the balcony to figure out what was happening. As soon as she looked down towards the lawn, she saw three piglings running around. White and pinkish in colour, the cute creatures were making noises and messing around with Mrs Samson's rocking chair. Tiny was unaware of their presence and was snoring away in the living room. Suddenly, the chair toppled over and Tiny woke up. By the time Laila came downstairs, Tiny had already scared the hell out of those piglings with its incessant barking, and the poor little things ran away. Laila then closed the gate and latched it properly. She set Mrs Samson's chair upright and went back to the kids upstairs.

Raju was now able to take better care of his wife and Harsh. Earlier, he would meet them thrice a week and for the rest of the time, he stayed in a rented room in the neighbourhood when not on duty. Sarita also started feeling better within a month because she had complete rest. Laila helped her out with almost everything while Sakhi was in control of the cooking. Raju regularly took Sarita for physical therapy at a charitable medical centre in the vicinity. Harsh was also able to concentrate better on his studies. All of them felt very grateful and indebted to Mrs Samson for her timely help.

After a span of two months, when Sarita showed marked improvement, they decided to return home. Although Mrs Samson told them that they could stay longer, they said that they didn't want to bother her further. The old lady accepted their decision, but only with a promise from them to return in case the slightest need arose.

> Some hearts are large enough
> To hold unending kindness
> And also, considerate enough
> To honour the other's self-respect.

The Growth Phase

A few months later, Laila was guided by Mrs Lalitha about the admissions notification for a teacher's training program. Mrs Samson thanked her friend. "That's so nice of you Lalitha. I've been telling Laila for a while now to check when the course begins. But this girl doesn't listen to me!"

Laila had been putting off the training for a while. Her reluctance stemmed from the fear of unintentionally neglecting the old lady. Mrs Samson said to her, "Sakhi is well-adjusted now. She takes good care of me. For how long do you want to wait?" Laila gave it a thought and later joined the course.

Once she took the plunge, her enthusiasm grew by the day. She was approaching forty, and all her peers at the institute were younger than her. Although she was mostly applauded for her dedication and zeal, occasional nasty comments pulled her down momentarily.

One such incident happened when she was attending a lecture and one of her seniors addressed her sarcastically as 'an elderly junior.' One of her peers objected but was silenced by the grins from a bunch of seniors. Laila was mature and poised and didn't react to the offensive comment. But when she left the class, she had tears in her eyes. In the evening, she narrated the incident to Ron. He told her to ignore such things. "Just focus on your coursework. If this happens again and you can't handle it, you can always report the bullying to higher authorities. Often, it's all that's required to silence the troublemakers. Just hold on to your confidence."

Simultaneously, another issue cropped up, and it didn't go unnoticed for long. Laila was reeling under the self-imposed guilt of not being able to give complete attention to Mrs Samson. Consequently, she started missing her classes. This led to her poor performance in the first semester. It struck her really hard.

Mrs Samson told her, "This is your own doing. When I tell you that Sakhi is taking good care of me and you need to focus on your classes, you don't listen! I've been warning you repeatedly about the consequences."

Laila felt disheartened. Nina visited over the weekend to cheer her up. Thanks to Nina's and Ron's efforts, Laila's zeal returned. They made her realize how blessed she was to be given a chance to pursue her dreams, given the conditions in which she had arrived in Delhi years ago.

"You've come so far based on your sincerity towards your job and dedication towards your growth as an individual. You've been continually crossing hurdles, achieving and accomplishing many wonderful things. This course will equip you with the right qualities to continue your services to underprivileged kids. You cannot take it lightly!" Ron cautioned.

Laila promised to pay attention to everyone's advice.

After a period of low-spiritedness, scenes of jubilation brightened the atmosphere when Ron got promoted to the rank of a Major. It was the high point of his life, and Laila was super happy for him. This change also helped melt away the uneasiness between Ron and his parents to a great extent. It was a moment of pride not only for them but for the entire village.

Laila too, put in her best effort for the subsequent semesters and scored well. She enrolled with an NGO to assist in educating children. In this way, she was able to reach more kids. Initially, she offered her services for two hours a day, because Mrs Samson was her priority. Soon, her stature strengthened to the level of a sought-after educator outside her social circle too. Mrs Samson was very happy with her progress.

Over a couple of years, Laila's role had changed from being a caretaker to a supervisor in the Samson household. Sakhi took over the major chunk of duties while Laila devoted more of her time to social work. Mrs Samson was always supportive of this change and motivated Laila to take up more responsibilities at the NGO.

Laila gradually climbed the ladder of success. Whenever off-duty, she would sit and talk to Mrs Samson for hours. She still baked sweet treats for the octogenarian and continued to clean the special bookshelf biweekly, no matter what. Although she had trained Sakhi well, weekend meals were always made by Laila.

Six months later, Raju's son, Harsh, got admission to a government medical college in Bangalore. It was a matter of great pride for Raju who had worked all his life as a driver to make ends meet. His wife, Sarita, had also worked at a fabric store as a saleswoman before Harsh was born. Both Raju and Sarita were beaming with joy when they visited Mrs Samson. They brought along a big box of chocolates and her favourite mango ice-cream.

Mrs Samson accepted the sweets and blessed Harsh with good wishes for success in life. She told Sarita, "In a few years when he becomes a doctor, he'll take care of all of us. We won't have to run here and there for treatment. I hope he will not charge us, Sarita!" Everyone burst into peals of laughter.

Raju said, "Madam, you have done so much for us. We are able to live comfortably because of you. You've been benevolent enough to sponsor his entire education. We are indebted to you."

"Come on Raju, all of you are like my children. I haven't done anything great. Now, have your ice-cream, or else it will melt!" Mrs Samson urged.

Laila gifted a personalised pen set to Harsh. She had seen him grow from a toddler to a responsible teenager, and she had always been appreciative of his dedication towards his studies. Nina also called to congratulate Harsh and the proud parents. Everyone enjoyed the evening and later Raju, Harsh and Sarita returned home.

Miles away, Jeffrey, Mrs Samson's grandson, was all grown up and had metamorphosed into a much more compassionate adult. He visited Mrs Samson once in two years. On one such trip, he brought along his close friend Elle. Elle was British, and her tastes matched those of Mrs Samson perfectly. They planned to stay for a month because Elle, a geologist by profession, was on a research trip.

The evenings in the Samson household were festive as tea was accompanied with cakes, pies, scones, sandwiches and so much more. The spread was lovingly prepared by Laila and Elle together.

Nina also visited during this time and got to meet Elle. Nina and Jeffrey were on much better terms now! There was no bullying, only decent conversation. "I learnt that you are a nurse," Elle said to Nina.

"Yes, I'm a trained ER nurse. I work in the Trauma Department of a hospital in Hyderabad."

"Have you ever thought of applying for a job in the UK? There's a lot of scope for nurses over there," an impressed Elle said to Nina.

"Actually, I haven't given it much thought till now. But a couple of my batchmates have gone there for work."

"No...no, don't give her such ideas. I will be left alone if she goes away and I must get her married soon," Laila interrupted.

Elle laughed and said, "Oh, then I won't!" Nina gave Laila a strange look and the focus shifted to food as Mrs Samson asked for some more chocolate sauce.

Later that night, Nina shared with Laila that she and Ravi were already thinking of applying for jobs abroad. They planned to shift after getting married. Laila was taken aback, but her maturity stopped her from reacting to this news. "So, my future will also be like Mrs Samson's," she thought to herself. Till midnight, she kept thinking about this matter. She was worried because she had seen Mrs Samson go through the never-ending pain of separation from her loved ones.

The next day, she talked to Ron about it. He understood her feelings but advised her to broaden her perspective. "You can't hold her back. Give her the freedom she seeks because there is nothing wrong with it. She wants new opportunities and if she's able to get a better deal, you shouldn't stop her. It's her and her partner's decision. Don't take things to heart. Give it some time. If she goes abroad and likes it there, you must accept it. If she feels that she wants to stay near you, she will return."

Laila understood his point and tried to stay as normal as possible despite the turmoil in her mind.

If you start, start wholeheartedly;
If you divert, divert confidently;
If you continue to dilly dally,
Your aims and accomplishments won't tally.

24

The New Couple

Nina was enjoying her extended vacation in Delhi and days later, her friend Ravi arrived. It was going to be his first meeting with Laila. Nina went to pick him up from the station with Raju. She was excited and nervous at the same time. Sitting under the orangish-grey evening sky on the lawn, Laila waited for them to arrive. Mrs Samson was seated comfortably beside her, in her rocking chair. She asked Laila, "Has Nina texted you? When are they expected to arrive?"

"Not yet, maybe the train is delayed."

"Looks like a dust storm is coming. Let's go inside."

At that moment, the bell rang and Nina arrived with Ravi. He was a tall, well-built young lad, and by the looks of it, they complemented each other exceptionally well. After they exchanged greetings, Laila ushered him in while Sakhi escorted Mrs Samson to the living room. Laila was a bit nervous. Time and again, she gestured Mrs Samson to do the talking as the eldest member of the family.

It was an hour-long interaction and the questions revolved around family background, job stability, future plans and so on. Ravi was fond of dogs, so he made Tiny sit by his side and gave him knick-knacks to eat. Tiny's immediate acceptance was one positive sign among many others noticed by Mrs Samson.

Later, Ravi left for his friend's place where he was going to stay for the next two days. Laila invited him for lunch the following day at a nearby restaurant where they finalised the plan to meet his parents. It was all very quick, and two months later, Ravi's parents flew down to Hyderabad and Laila also went there. It was a formal meeting to fix Nina and Ravi's marriage. Although the date wasn't decided there, they agreed upon solemnising the marriage the following year.

Laila returned home in a day's time. While en route to Delhi, she talked to Ron about the developments. Ron asked her, "So, what's your opinion of Ravi's family?"

"They seemed very reserved. His mother did all the talking which was centred around the wedding plan. She elaborated on a few compulsory rituals which they want us to arrange for. She wasn't interested in talking much about their family and relatives."

"Oh, what about Ravi's father and siblings?"

"His father was busy talking to Ravi all the time. His younger sister couldn't come although she had planned to. And I noticed something peculiar; Ravi suddenly seemed like an introvert. It was not the case when he had visited us in Delhi."

"Maybe he was conscious in front of his parents. You want me to enquire?"

"I don't know; might as well ask Nina first. You know her temper. She already told me that I don't have a choice!"

"Okay, don't worry. Do let me know if I can help in any way. Got some work now. Bye."

"Bye, Ron."

One evening, when Ron and Laila were on a call, Ron told her, "I'll be heading home on annual leave in a month's time. Are you planning to renovate your house any time soon?" For a long time, Laila had been saving money to renovate her house in the village. She had plans to relocate there sometime later in life. "I mean, you're relatively free, you can spare a week's time. You even have the finances to take up the renovation," he continued.

"Not this year, I must plan for Nina's wedding."

He offered to share the financial responsibility but Laila politely declined.

A short while later, she realised that some changes would have to be made to the house for Nina's wedding too. She called Ron and discussed the matter with him. They finalized a plan: Laila and Nina would go to the village with Ron for four to five days and work on the renovation plan. Ron would follow up during the month he planned to spend there.

With just a few days left to leave for Dehradun, an idea struck Ron. He suggested that Ravi could also accompany them to the village. It would give them more time to interact with him. Laila loved the suggestion and conveyed it to Nina.

Laila had informed Mrs Samson about the probable trip early on. Just a day before they were to leave, Mrs Samson transferred a lump sum into Laila's account. Laila told her, "Madam, you seem to have transferred thrice the bonus amount this year! Anyway, I will transfer the excess back to you."

"No, it was intentional."

"Why so, Madam?"

"Just felt like being generous. Nina's wedding is coming up and you are planning to renovate the house in the village. This money will come in handy. And mind you, this is not a gift…just your earnings."

When it was time, Ron arrived to pick Laila up for the onward journey. He was already in the good books of Mrs Samson. She was always excited to meet him whenever he visited. As soon as he entered, he said, "Good afternoon, Madam. How are you doing today?"

Mrs Samson nudged Laila, signalling to help her stand up. "Good afternoon, Major Sharma. I'm doing great. It's so good to see you." He knelt and kissed her hand and helped her sit comfortably.

Laila had tears in her eyes and a proud smile spread across her face. After spending an hour with Mrs Samson, he said, "I think we should make a move now." Laila nodded and soon, they left for the station. They were to meet Nina and Ravi at the Dehradun Station directly. On the train, Ron surprised Laila with a beautiful gold chain. "I've realized my dream and you've been by my side through all my struggles. I wanted to share my happiness with you." Laila became emotional and her tears conveyed more than any words ever could.

When they reached their destination, Nina was already waiting there with Ravi. The love birds were busy sipping hot tea when Laila playfully patted Nina's back. Nina turned around and both hugged each other excitedly.

Nina introduced Ravi to Ron. Since childhood, she had addressed Ron as 'Ron Uncle.' "Ravi, meet Uncle Ron," she said.

"Nina, I hope you know that it's Major Ron now!" Ron said and they all started laughing. The men shook hands and exchanged pleasantries after which they boarded a bus to head to the village.

It was a fun trip for the new couple, but Laila and Ron surely had the added responsibility of drawing inferences on the alliance.

New relationships are like fresh fruits;
They are luscious-looking;
Work on them to create something worthy,
Even after the wrinkles have set in!

25

Renovation?

Once in the village, Laila and Nina went home while Ron went to his place. Ravi accompanied Laila and Nina for the day. As soon as he entered the house, Ravi began coughing as he was allergic to dust. The house had been locked for a long time.

"Why don't you take a chair and sit outside till we clean the house," Laila suggested, as she began the dusting. Nina decided to take Ravi along to get some groceries. She excitedly showed him around on the way there. By the time they returned, the house had been spotlessly cleaned.

Then, Nina and Ravi took over the kitchen. Both were great cooks. Living away from home had made them so. Their meal consisted of fragrant cumin rice, a lentil and vegetable stew and spiced yoghurt. Laila was very impressed by their efforts. She could smell the fragrance of their compatibility.

Things moved as planned till Laila's maternal relatives learned about the probable renovation. Five middle-aged ladies came knocking on their door when Laila was alone at home. At first, they appeared calm. Laila ushered them in, but as soon as the conversation started, she realised they were there to talk about the ownership of the house!

Laila went into the kitchen and messaged Ron to come ASAP. The women were Laila's mother's sisters and the house was jointly owned by her mother and maternal grandfather. When her grandparents were alive, their decision to give the house to Laila's mother was unopposed. Now, the situation had changed. The paperwork, however, probably hadn't been done, so things weren't in Laila's favour either. Her aunts seemingly took advantage of this and showed up asking for their share.

Ron arrived within a few minutes, and as expected of a gentleman, he greeted the ladies. They accepted his greetings but raised their eyebrows and whispered among themselves. They had no idea why Ron was there, till Laila introduced him as a friend.

Unaware of their togetherness, one of the ladies whispered into Laila's ear, "We'll come in the evening." Laila stopped them and insisted that the issue be discussed in his presence.

As Laila explained the situation to Ron, one of her aunts interrupted. "You don't have the full picture, Laila. Keep quiet and let me explain." Laila felt offended but out of respect, she let the lady elaborate.

Ron signalled Laila to stay calm during the conversation. Then he asked the ladies, "I can understand your point, but why didn't you all discuss this earlier?"

At this moment, Nina and Ravi returned home. They had been out to the local market. Nina didn't know any of those ladies because she had spent only the early years of her childhood in the village. She found the conversation offensive and the attitude of the aunts domineering. "But this is our mother's house!" she interrupted. Ravi indicated to Nina that it was not right to voice her opinion at that moment. Laila asked Nina to go to her room.

A discussion ensued but there wasn't any solution. The ladies left, but not before warning Laila to refrain from making any changes to the house. No one had expected the aunts to visit. Once the ladies had left, Ron asked Laila to tell him the details. Of all the information that she shared with him, the most important bit was when she said, "Once, Mummy had mentioned about some important papers kept safely at my maternal grandparents' home. I don't know whether those are the ownership documents."

"Then, let's go and check at your grandparents' place."

"It's not so easy. My grandparents expired two years after Nina's father's death. And my uncle who lived in the house with my grandparents never entertained me or my mother."

It was a tense situation and time was running out. If the matter was left unattended, it would mean that eventually Laila and Nina would lose the house.

The excitement with which all four of them had reached the village had completely fizzled out by then. Over evening tea, when they were discussing the issue, they heard someone scream suddenly. They rushed outside to check. There was a chaotic crowd at a short distance from their house. Ron and Ravi went to see what had happened. As soon as they reached the spot, Ravi jumped right into the middle of the crowd as if to pounce on something. A shocked Nina also rushed to the spot and was, in turn, followed by Laila.

In Ravi's hands lay a child with profuse cranial bleeding. It was a terrible head injury. The child had probably fallen off a bike and his head had got smashed by a rock. Both Nina and Ravi were well trained to handle such situations. They acted swiftly to arrest the bleeding and brought the child back to consciousness. The poor boy was writhing in pain. Ron borrowed a neighbour's bike and they took the child to a medical facility where first-aid was administered. Thankfully, the child was stable, but the doctor advised further investigation at a hospital.

The child's parents said, "There is no hospital nearby, nor do we have the funds to get the tests done."

"Seeing the gravity of the injury, these tests are essential to rule out internal damage. It can be life-threatening if left untreated," Nina cautioned them.

"I'll arrange for the tests and will foot the bill too," Ron offered.

The child was taken to a hospital, about fifty kilometres away. Luckily, there was no internal injury and the child was safe. The parents thanked Ron and the others for their timely help.

After a tough evening, when they reached home at night, Laila told Ron to have dinner with them. Post dinner, when he and Ravi were about to leave, someone knocked on their door. It was fairly uncommon to have late-night visitors in the village. However, since all of them were together, they decided to open the door. If it would have been just the women, they wouldn't have.

At the door, Ron was surprised to see one of Laila's aunts. He asked her the reason for her visit. With tears in her eyes, she said, "Please let me in, I can't stand here and talk." Ron suspected some foul play, so he tried to convince her that he wouldn't be able to let her in. But she persisted and pleaded. He let her in, and she approached Laila.

All of them were alert, so Ravi and Nina tried to protect Laila. Suddenly, she fell at Laila's feet and said, "I'm sorry, I'm so sorry. You are good people. Please forgive me." Laila told her to get up and Nina helped her.

They asked her to explain herself. She revealed that the child whom they had helped in the evening was her grandchild. All four of them were surprised. Then, she told them something which hit them like a bolt out of the blue.

"My sisters and I know that Laila's condition has improved ever since she started working in Delhi. Nina is also doing well, while all of us here in the village are still struggling financially. Had Laila's mother not been widowed twice, our father wouldn't have given away the house to her," she said. She ran out of breath and was given water. She continued, "I thought that Laila and Nina didn't need the property anymore, and it should be divided equally among all of us. Thus, I supported my sisters in the decision not to forgo our right to a share of the property. Now, I have realised that we were being unjust."

What she said next stunned all of them. "The original papers are with our eldest sister."

Later, when she went away, out of sheer relief, Ron said, "Interesting! So, the papers do exist."

Property and money often ruin relationships.
When scarcity and abundance are placed on the weighing scale,
Only social conscience can equalise and fix.

26

Unanticipated

Ron and Laila were sorted and mature individuals. They gauged the intensity of her aunts' insecurities. After all, Laila had made the move from the village to the city to improve the financial situation of her family. Presently, she had a firm footing, compared to her aunts. Laila decided that she would take time to think before proceeding with the renovation. She wanted to make peace with her aunts first, as they were the only people in the village whom she could call family. At the same time, she was aware that she could not give her house away at any cost because she considered it as a security for her old age. Both Laila and Ron were of the same opinion. The next day, they called the ladies for another discussion to resolve the problem at hand.

Four of her aunts arrived while the one who had visited the previous night didn't come. "Suguna Aunty didn't come? Is her grandson, okay?" Laila asked.

One of the ladies replied, "Yes, he's fine. Thankfully, some good people helped her family and the child is out of danger."

Another aunt said, "Yes. Suguna herself isn't feeling well so she hasn't come. But tell me, what have you decided?"

Laila gathered that her aunt, Suguna, hadn't shared any information with her sisters. "I have always respected all of you. I am in no position to decide because I have no proof regarding the ownership of this house," she explained.

The eldest of the ladies was quick to say, "Good that you've realized your mistake. We wouldn't have allowed you to walk away with our share anyway!"

Ron and Laila looked at each other and shared a moment of surprise.

The lady continued, "You've migrated to the city; you earn so much. It's visible in the way you dress, your footwear, and your jewellery! Meanwhile, our families still struggle to make ends meet."

Laila expected the conversation to end on this note since she had made it amply clear that she wouldn't be making any changes to the house. But the ladies shook her up when they told her that before returning to the city, she ought to give them the house keys. This infuriated Laila, and she was about to speak up when there was a knock on the door. Ron signalled her to open the door because he didn't want her to speak up at that moment, as it would only complicate the matter.

"Suguna, come. They've been asking for you!" said one of the elderly ladies. As Suguna entered, she blessed Laila with a pat on her shoulder. Her sisters were astonished and exchanged strange expressions. One of the ladies made some space for her and asked her to sit by her side. Suguna boldly sat next to Laila. She had a couple of papers rolled in her saree. She untied the knot which held the papers and handed them over to Laila.

The other ladies recognized the papers and were in utter shock. One of them nearly fell out of her chair and shouted, "How dare you, Suguna! This is our share; this girl and her half-sister can't get what is ours."

"The truth is that we don't have any share in this house. I request all of you to not rob this kind-hearted girl of her rightfully deserved share," Suguna pleaded. She then narrated how Laila, Nina, Ron and Ravi had helped her grandson in his hour of need.

It was introspection time for the elderly ladies. They realised that Laila had refrained from disrespecting them, knowing fully well that they were lying to her. Instead, she reciprocated their unfair behaviour with calm. She wanted to preserve her relationships with her aunts and they realised it soon. They apologized to her. She had tears in her eyes as she said, "If I can help unknown, underprivileged kids in the city, why won't I help my own family!"

The umbrella of kindness is huge;
It can protect many from getting drenched.
When shared to take the cause forward
It leaves challenges feeling challenged.

27

The Race Against Time

Owing to sensible handling of the situation, Laila and Ron were able to settle the matter. But now they were left with very little time to plan and arrange for the renovations. Although Ron's brother was going to oversee the process, the planning and finalization was Laila's responsibility. Nina wanted two additional rooms, a guest room, and a study. However, Laila wanted just one with a small additional washroom. She liked open spaces and didn't want to do away with the veranda.

Eventually, Laila had the final word. Ron, his brother, and Ravi went to meet a contractor. Their plan hit a roadblock when the proposed expenses overshot the budget by almost fifty percent. Ron was ready to help Laila with the expenses, but she decided to just get the washroom built along with an aluminium shed over the open space. She said that the room could be built later on, and temporary tenting would suffice for the wedding.

The final decisions were made and the plan was chalked out. Later that day, Laila prepared a feast and all five of them spent an enjoyable evening. Then the boys returned to Ron's place. This was the first stress-free night for Laila in a long, long time.

The next morning, Ron's parents invited the youngsters for lunch. Although Laila had paid them a visit right after her arrival, they wanted to spend more time with Laila and Nina. They agreed. Laila prepared a delicious sweet dish for all, which she took along.

Ron's father was diabetic so she made sure to cook a separate portion for him which had a low-calorie sweetener that she had brought from Delhi. They were surprised at this version of the sweet dish and Ron's father gave her money as a prize for her efforts. Over the years, she had started caring for Ron's parents too. She used to call them often and made sure that she remained connected to them. His parents had also, more or less, accepted her as a family member.

As always, Ron's mother did brook upon the topic of marriage. Only, this time, she talked to Laila about it. In a very soft, motherly tone, she said to Laila, "My child, we know that both of you share a surreal level of togetherness and we are happy about it. But, why don't you get married? Believe me, your relationship will only grow into a more beautiful one. We know that you have a level of commitment towards Mrs Samson and we respect your thought process, but you should also think about yourself and Ron. Do give it a thought, my dear!"

She gifted a gold ring to Laila and made her wear it. Laila hugged her and her embrace conveyed her feelings. She had kept it for Ron's bride, and in her heart, she felt satisfied while placing it on Laila's finger.

**A heartfelt wish, a heart-warming gesture,
For elders, is no less an investiture.**

28

Out of Sorts

Lately, Laila had been feeling an unusual kind of pain in her knees. Earlier, she never experienced knee pain. "I've been managing with ointments and crepe bandage for the pain and discomfort. Now, the intensity of pain has increased. What should I do?" she asked Nina.

"Do hot fomentation regularly, and take an over-the-counter analgesic if the pain is intolerable."

"Do you think it's something serious?"

"It's just knee pain. And you can walk, right? Why are you so worried?"

"No, I was just asking!"

Nina didn't realise that Laila was holding back something. However, the pain settled and she felt better. She got busy with daily activities at home and at the NGO. One day, during Women's Day celebrations at the NGO, she was invited to deliver a speech on the podium. As she was climbing the stairs, she heard a cracking sound in one of her knees. She felt a bit of stiffness that very moment, but she managed to reach the podium and delivered the speech. Afterwards, she thought, "Those stairs were higher than regular stairs and may have caused the discomfort."

Later that evening, when she was boarding a rickshaw to head back home, she felt a sharp pain in her knee and could not move her right leg. As a result, she fell on the road. A few bystanders helped her. They made her sit on the pavement. She requested them to arrange an auto rickshaw to reach home which was just ten minutes away.

When Laila reached home, she was limping. Sakhi, who was cleaning the gate, asked her, "What happened, Didi?" She could make out that Laila had met with an accident as was evident from her soiled clothes and broken sandals. She supported Laila and took her inside the living room towards the couch. After making Laila sit comfortably, she got water for her. Then, she cleaned the bruises and applied an antiseptic ointment.

Mrs Samson was reading messages on her cell phone, lying comfortably in her bed, when she said to Sakhi, "Laila should have come home by now. Call her to find out when she's coming."

"Didi reached just now. She's in the living room."

"Okay. Remind her that I have my follow-up at the hospital tomorrow so that she can get the papers ready in time."

"Sure, Madam. I will let her know."

When Laila didn't turn up to fetch the medical files, Mrs Samson called out to her anxiously. "Laila, what have you been busy with? Come fast." By then, an hour had passed and she was able to walk by herself but was still uncomfortable. On seeing Laila's condition, Mrs Samson exclaimed, "O Lord! What happened to you, Laila? Looks like you had a fall."

Laila nodded. "Yes, I fell while boarding a rickshaw."

"Sit here, don't stand for long, you seem to have injured your joint," said Mrs Samson, as she held her hand to help her sit down.

Meanwhile, Sakhi got her some turmeric milk, the age-old home remedy used in almost every Indian house. Laila didn't feel like drinking it. She wasn't a big fan of milk, but Mrs Samson made sure that she gulped it down. That day, Laila slept in a room on the ground floor as she could not climb the stairs.

The whole night she was tense. Although she knew that her pain was from the fall, she was anxious. She was constantly reminded that she had trouble climbing the stairs earlier in the day too. She got a call from Nina just before midnight and she briefed her about it. Nina assessed her condition and advised her to see an orthopaedic doctor.

Laila was constantly likening her condition to that of Sarita's. She didn't mention it to anyone but was fearful. After all, Sarita had been suffering immensely due to arthritis. The poor lady wasn't even able to go about her daily activities. She was on strong medication and suffered their side effects. Sometimes, she would cry when Laila called to check on her.

Seeing Laila's condition, Mrs Samson told her to reschedule her cardiology appointment at the hospital for the next week. In a couple of days, Laila felt better and resumed work at the NGO. Later, she took Mrs Samson for her check-up too.

Laila wanted to put off visiting an orthopaedic, but she had started feeling a slight and constant pain throughout the day, each day. So, she booked an appointment with a doctor at a nearby charitable hospital. She had the money to go to a private clinic but she knew it would be heavy on her pocket if further investigation was advised. Besides, the doctors at the charitable hospital had a good reputation. They were known for their selfless service to the not-so-wealthy class.

She went for the appointment, and the doctor prescribed some x-rays to be done. He told Laila, "You've started to develop osteoarthritis." As soon as she heard this, a strange current ran down her body. Seeing a marked change in her reaction, the doctor asked, "Are you okay?"

"Did you just say arthritis, Doctor?"

"No, I said osteoarthritis. It is pretty common these days. In simple terms, your knee joints are showing signs of wear and tear. There is considerable friction which is causing discomfort and pain. The good news is that it is in the initial stage, and luckily there has been no damage from the fall. Otherwise, it would have complicated the situation." He prescribed medication and told her to do a few exercises every day.

A relieved Laila reached home in high spirits. The fear that had stemmed from witnessing Sarita's condition had fizzled out. She narrated it all to Mrs Samson. After hearing her out, Mrs Samson said, "Oh, my child, if you were so worried, why didn't you talk to me? I'm not a doctor but could have helped in allaying your fear to some extent at least."

Laila smiled and then she joyously went into the kitchen to bake some muffins for Mrs Samson.

Over a period of six months, during which Laila religiously followed her exercise schedule and took her medication, her condition improved. She returned to her active self as her pain had almost gone, although she kept her activities light.

Fear becomes dearer if you are the anxious kind.
Even minor issues appear threatening until clarity unwinds.

29

Care and Concern

Age doesn't spare anyone, and that proved true in the case of Mrs Lalitha, an old, dear friend of Mrs Samson. She was five years older than Mrs Samson and had three kids, two of whom had settled abroad. They were an upper-middle-class family. Her son and daughter-in-law, who stayed with her, worked as software engineers. She was in and out of hospitals often due to end-stage kidney disease. One day, she passed away.

Mrs Samson was very close to her, and Laila always felt indebted to her as Mrs Lalitha had been instrumental in encouraging her to pursue further studies. Raju took both of them to Mrs Lalitha's place. By then, Mrs Samson had become very frail, and the incident turned out to be emotionally draining for her. She cried profusely when she saw her friend lying in a refrigerated case, draped in a white, silk saree with flowers all around. Mrs Samson took an exquisite embroidered shawl and placed it over her body as a mark of love and respect. Mrs Lalitha was very fond of pearls, so Mrs Samson handed a string of pearls to Laila to offer her dear friend as a mark of respect. Laila said to Mrs Samson, "Madam, Raju will take you home and I'll come after attending the funeral service."

The old lady was far from convinced. "No, what are you saying? I'm not going home."

It had been a long day for Mrs Samson, and Mrs Lalitha's son and daughter-in-law were also concerned about her health. As soon as the rituals began, they insisted that Mrs Samson pay obeisance and then be taken home in time.

On the way home, their car broke down. Its battery had been giving trouble for the past year, and Raju had often got it repaired and recharged. However, he knew that it needed to be replaced. He had mentioned this to Mrs Samson, but she told him to get it done once her son arrived. Her elder son, Eric, was to arrive in a week's time.

Now, they were left stranded on the road in the scorching heat. To add to their woes, somehow, the front doors got stuck. Laila had to tug forcefully and incessantly till she was able to open them. Raju walked up to an autorickshaw stand and after much persuasion, he managed to book a ride for both the ladies. Mrs Samson's house was in an interior area of Delhi and the traffic jam in the adjoining areas made drivers decline rides to the busy stretch.

Mrs Samson and Laila reached home after a while, but Raju was still stranded as he waited for a crane to arrive so that the car could be ferried to the service station. After a harrowing three-hour ordeal, Raju returned home. "Can you give me a cup of tea and some medicine for my headache? I'm exhausted," he requested Laila.

"Of course, sit here!" She turned on the cooler and first gave him water to drink. He was all wet from perspiration and complained of tiredness.

He took a day off and then checked with the service station. He was told that the car battery was dead. When he told Mrs Samson about it, she said, "Let bhaiya come, he'll be here in a week and then you can get the replacement done."

Mrs Samson was an independent lady. Mostly, all the decision-making was done by her, but when it came to automobiles she depended on her sons. Raju obediently said, "Okay, Madam. Since the car is at the service station, and I have no work here, can I take two days off? Actually, Harsh wants to visit the ancient temple in our village. He has been wanting to go there for quite some time now." Mrs Samson conceded to his request.

A week later, her elder son arrived. Raju went to receive him at the airport in a taxi. He asked Raju, "Why this taxi? What happened to the car?"

Raju explained the situation to him in detail. When he came to know that his mother had to wait on the road in the scorching heat, he was very upset. When Raju told him that such situations cropped up repeatedly over the last year, he told Raju, "Don't get the battery replaced. We'll buy a new car. This one is twelve years old. Make arrangements to sell it. And most important, don't tell Mom. I want it to be a surprise for her."

At home, it was an emotional reunion for the mother-son duo. As years passed by and her health deteriorated, Mrs Samson became emotionally weak and so did her sons. She hugged Eric and said, "You make me wait for so long. Try to plan at least one trip a year. I'm growing old. I have little strength left. I feel that I'm left with little time!"

He wiped off her tears and said, "Oh, Mom, don't even think this way. You are just going to turn eighty. You have a long, long way to go. And you've always believed that age is just a number. Come on, Mom! Give me a smile now, please!"

Mrs Samson smiled, and as soon as Raju brought the luggage in, he said, "Let me open my suitcase. Jeffry has sent a special gift for you and it is perishable."

He struggled with the zipper of his suitcase which got stuck midway. After an intense session of pulling and pushing, he managed to open it. A fragrance spread across the room and Mrs Samson remarked, "Over the years, I've noticed that whenever you or, for that matter, any foreign returnee opens a suitcase, pleasing fragrance wafts through the air." As he pulled out a beautifully wrapped cake and handed it over to Mrs Samson, he said mischievously, "Here you go, Mom. Elle made this vanilla-walnut cake for you, and your grandson wrapped it up with all his love!"

Laila, who was standing beside Mrs Samson, helped her unwrap the cake and brought a knife to cut it. It was delicious and they all enjoyed it. Elle and Jeffrey had also included a note which read, "Dear Grandmother, Congratulations! Stay healthy, happy and super-cool as you turn eighty in the coming week."

A birthday celebration had been planned by her son well in advance. He wanted to take Mrs Samson, her friends, his extended family and Irene's parents to a fine-dining restaurant for a cosy brunch. However, due to Mrs Lalitha's demise, the old lady wasn't keen on a celebration. She wanted to keep it a low-key affair at home, without friends and decorations. He understood her feelings and didn't want to disturb her. He had booked a brand-new luxury car as her birthday gift so he went ahead with just that.

On the eve of Mrs Samson's eightieth birthday, the new car arrived. He told Laila to bring his mother outside so that he could give her the surprise. Laila went inside and told Mrs Samson, "Madam, it's very pleasant outside. Let me take you to the lawn and you can enjoy the nice weather in your rocking chair."

"No, I'm tired. I already sat outside in the sun for my dose of Vitamin D in the morning."

"Madam, believe me, you'll feel rejuvenated. It is so pleasant outside. Please come for my sake!"

It wasn't new for Mrs Samson to be coaxed into some light activity every now and then, after her paralytic attack. Although reluctant she agreed. Outside, her son was ready with the car and a huge bouquet of red roses. He had got a special licence plate number, 8080, to commemorate the occasion. When Mrs Samson was led outside, all of them started clapping and took her towards the porch. She was speechless for a moment and then said, "No, no, no...what is this? Why did you do this, Eric?"

"Mom, this is your birthday gift from both your sons."

"Why this luxury car? I hardly travel these days. No, no...this is not right."

"Mom, the old sedan was too low and uncomfortable for you. This SUV has comfortable seating and great shock absorbers. Whenever you want, Raju can take you out for a drive. It is for your convenience. Enjoy it and bless us so that we can be of some help to you."

The old lady had tears of joy and contentment in her eyes. She was happy to know that her kids thought so much about her. She then kissed his forehead and said, "Thank you, my child. God bless!"

The next morning, everyone was in a celebratory mood. It was raining phone calls, and birthday wishes poured in from friends and family. Laila and Sakhi prepared a lavish breakfast spread which consisted of blueberry muffins, banoffee pie, fruit salad, porridge, honey toast, etc. They had invited two of Mrs Samson's best friends to uplift her mood. Nina surprised her lovely DG right in the morning. She flew down to Delhi just for a few hours. It touched the old lady's heart.

Laila had been secretly knitting a blanket for Mrs Samson at night in her room upstairs. She knew that Mrs Samson loved knitted shawls, as she had shown her a few that she had made in her youth. Laila waited for the formal celebrations to conclude. In the evening, she gifted the hand-knitted blanket to Mrs Samson in her room.

Laila had taken six months to knit the beautiful cream and brown-coloured piece. Mrs Samson was so happy to receive the gift that she kissed Laila's hand and made her sit by her side. She took a closer look and appreciated the cables and chevron pattern on the blanket. "I learned to knit over the internet. First, I practised on smaller squares and then I started making this one for you," Laila told her.

A beaming Mrs Samson told her, "Oh, my darling Laila, you've given the perfect ending to this day. I love it. Thank you so much. Generally, I've seen old ladies knit for their grandchildren. But you've given me this gift and it makes me feel really special."

Laila switched off the lights, put on the night lamp in Mrs Samson's room and proceeded to the second floor to sleep.

A couple of days passed by. One evening, when Laila had returned from the NGO, Mrs Samson's son was taking a stroll on the lawn. He saw Laila disembark with great difficulty from a rickshaw. "Laila, do you have a knee issue? I saw your discomfort," he said.

"Yes, Sir, I have osteoarthritis. But it's not too bad, although getting on and off a rickshaw sometimes gives me a little trouble. I generally try to travel by an auto rickshaw but sometimes they are not available."

The next morning, over breakfast he told his mother, "Mom, I've been urging Laila for the last couple of years to learn driving. She doesn't seem to listen to me. Travelling in a rickshaw is difficult and dangerous considering the condition of her knees."

Laila was not surprised about Eric's concern for her. His line of thought about the staff at the Samson house had changed over the years. He had become more compassionate towards them. After all, they were the ones who were constantly around his mother, and they took really good care of her.

Mrs Samson told Laila, "Listen to bhaiya. He's right. You must learn to drive. I'll give you an interest-free loan to buy a scooter. It will make commuting safer and comfortable for you." Laila kept quiet all through the conversation, neither denying nor agreeing to it.

An empathetic glance, a sincere effort,
A warm embrace, a word of concern,
Amplify the message of heartfelt care,
And seal the bond of affection.

30

Nina's Wedding

"Deck up this area really well because the groom's relatives will be sitting here for the function. I want red and pink roses for the garlands, and marigold and jasmine flowers for the decoration," Laila instructed the contractor who had been hired for the wedding arrangements. Ron had taken a week off to be a part of the wedding festivities.

Laila, Nina, Ron, and his brother, were all busy with something or the other. They were pushing for the arrangements to be completed before the arrival of Ravi and his family.

"Laila, did you decide on gulab jamun or rasmalai for dessert? I can't seem to remember," Ron said, as he was finalising the menu with the caterer.

Laila shouted from the veranda, "Gulab jamun, and in addition, we need twenty boxes, two hundred and fifty grams each of motichoor laddoos to distribute post the wedding ceremony."

Nina was busy giving instructions to the tailor concerning last-minute alterations to her wedding dress. "Can we do away with the extra veil? It is so cumbersome to carry this embellished piece," she said to Laila.

Laila screamed at the top of her voice. "Don't even think of doing it. It is essential. Your mother-in-law has sent it." "Modern girls," she murmured. Ron patted her lovingly on her head and told her to take things easy.

She continued, "No, seriously! All the neighbours and elderly relatives will be there. This girl wants shortcuts everywhere."

Suddenly, there was a spark and the lights went off. Ron rushed outside to check. The electrician told him, "A fuse went off while connecting the decorative lights to the mains. I'll get it changed, don't worry, Sir, the power will be restored in half an hour."

The work was stalled for an hour forcing everyone to take rest.

On the second day of preparations, around ten mattresses, numerous sheets and pillows arrived, loaded on two rickshaws. On inspecting them Laila said, "Oh no, these look dirty! How will our guests use them?"

"There's no time to get them changed, the guests will start arriving tomorrow evening. Take them in and we'll see what we can do," Ron suggested.

An unwilling Laila accepted his suggestion. Ron told his brother to bring some bedsheets from home. Within two hours, the mattresses were laid out and sheets neatly spread over to make things look perfect. Laila was relieved when she saw the set up.

Rita had also arrived at her parents' place to attend Nina's wedding. Her sons had started walking by this time. They kept her on her feet, feeding them, cleaning up after them, searching for their toys, and doing everything else one could imagine. In the evening, when the kids had gone to sleep giving her a breather, she visited Laila for a short while.

Rita took along a box of sweets. It was a speciality of the town where she lived. Her husband was busy with work so he couldn't come. Actually, he was a person of reserved nature and hardly visited his in-laws once or twice a year. But everyone at Ron's place was okay with this because they knew that Rita was happy and that he was a good human being.

Rita took Laila into the kitchen and lovingly handed over Nina's wedding gift. She chose to do it in the kitchen to maintain privacy. Laila was surprised to see that it was a beautiful piece of fine jewellery. "What is this? Such an expensive gift, Rita! I can't take this from you. We don't accept such hefty gifts from younger sisters," Laila told her.

Rita hugged her and said, "Nina is like a daughter to me. Keep it safely in the almirah before anyone sees it. You can give it to her later in the night." This gesture left Laila teary-eyed.

The following morning, a prayer was organized to mark the beginning of the celebrations. All the ladies from the neighbourhood came for the prayer. There was Ron's family, and Laila's relatives also came from the neighbouring village.

Ravi arrived with his parents in the evening and a few of his relatives followed late at night. Laila had made arrangements for dinner and everyone settled down. The wedding was to be solemnised the following day. A small pre-wedding ceremony was also planned for at noon.

Laila was waiting for some special guests, so time and again, she went towards the gate to check. Actually, it was Nina's paternal uncle and his family. He was the only person from Nina's deceased father's family who had regularly been in touch with Laila throughout the years, to check on their wellbeing. Nina's other relatives never really bothered to enquire about her. Perhaps they didn't want to be burdened with the added responsibility. Laila had tried to connect Nina with them on many occasions but failed. She tried her best to preserve the bond between Nina and her relatives but it hadn't worked out. As a result, once the child grew up, it was only this uncle whom Nina knew as her paternal family. She was also excited to see them.

A young lady, almost Laila's age arrived at their gate. Draped in a beautiful green saree accessorised with gold jewellery and with white flowers in her hair, she waited at the gate. Moments later, her husband followed holding a tiny girl in his arms and along with him came Uncle Karthik. Laila rushed towards the gate. She touched his feet and ushered them in. He introduced Laila to his son, daughter-in-law, and granddaughter.

"Nina! See who's come," Laila said.

Nina was in the veranda with Ravi's parents. She went towards them although she couldn't recognize her uncle because they had hardly met once or twice. But as soon as her uncle said, "Nina, my child. You look so pretty," she recognized his voice and warmly greeted all of them.

Laila introduced them to everyone, especially Ravi and his parents. Ron also came forward to meet them. He touched Uncle Karthik's feet and shook hands with his son. As soon as he saw the young lady, he froze for a moment. His smile and greeting had just reached halfway when a tiny toddler ran right across, stunning all of them. Ron turned around and went inside quickly.

The priest arrived and the ceremony started. There was a fragrance of marigold and jasmine all around and the guests were ringing the small bells given to them. Interestingly, Ron's parents looked equally shocked when they were introduced to Uncle Karthik's daughter-in-law. The interaction, however, was limited to customary greetings. The bride and groom completed the prayer and an hour later, after lunch, the wedding ceremony began. Amidst the chanting of holy mantras, the hour-long ceremony was completed, and the guests showered the newlywed couple with flower petals.

Later in the evening, the guests had dinner amidst discussions of how well Laila had planned the wedding. The neighbours left after dinner while a few relatives stayed the night. Ravi and Nina left at night for their home along with the parents. They were to visit a holy shrine on the way back home.

Early the next morning, Uncle Karthik approached Laila while she was sitting all alone and sipping coffee. "Laila, I'm so proud of you. You have always fulfilled your responsibilities towards Nina. Right from childhood, you've taken good care of her. You educated her and made her stand on her feet. And now you've married her off well," he said, handing over an envelope to her.

"Uncle, what is this?" she asked, as she opened the envelope. There was a substantial amount of cash in there. A surprised Laila tried to return it. "I can't take this. You already gave Nina her gift yesterday. Why this?"

"Most members of our family, including my brothers and sisters, never acknowledged their responsibility towards Nina. Even I couldn't do much due to my financial condition. It is my duty to contribute towards her wedding expenses," he told Laila, teary-eyed.

Laila held his hand and said, "You came along with your family. This is more than enough for us. Didn't you see how proud Nina was to introduce her cousin and his wife to her in-laws? You've given her the best gift!"

He insisted and Laila had no option but to accept the gift, as she saw the immense satisfaction on his face.

At around 8:00 a.m., Ron visited Laila. It was time to settle the bills and make the final payments to the decorators, caterers, etc. When he came, Uncle Karthik and his family were having breakfast, after which they were to leave. He greeted everyone. Laila asked him to join them for breakfast. Ron said that he had already had his breakfast as he entered one of the rooms. Laila sensed some uneasiness, especially between Ron and Nina's sister-in-law. However, they left a few hours later and Laila got busy with the financial settlement.

In the evening, she went around the neighbourhood distributing sweets she had specially ordered. It was customary to share one's happiness in this manner on such occasions in the village.

With a wedding to organise, how can the hosts relax?
One can't afford to let a single lamp run out of wax.

31

The Aftereffects

After Nina's wedding, Ron's parents invited Laila for dinner. She took beautiful silk sarees for Ron's mother and sister, shawls for his father and brother, and chocolates for Rita's sons. They were hesitant to accept the gifts initially, but at her request, they did so. Rita and her mother had prepared a delicious cottage-cheese gravy, fragrant rice, fresh ground chutney, lentil stew with vegetables and a delicious rice pudding for dessert. They were Laila's favourite dishes. Laila was extremely touched by the special efforts they had put in. Ron took her to a corner and asked teasingly, "What about my gift? You didn't get anything for me!"

Laila laughed and said, "I'm glad to know that you expected one. Finally, you are learning to acknowledge your wishes. Your gift has been delivered at Mrs Samson's house in Delhi. I couldn't get it delivered here. So, you'll get it on your way back."

Ron gave her a contented smile saying, "Thanks, I was joking. I already have your friendship as my gift!" Laila blushed.

When Ron escorted her back home at night, Laila asked him casually, "Ron, can I ask you something? Have you met Uncle Karthik's daughter-in-law earlier? Don't get me wrong, but I just felt that you were uncomfortable meeting her."

"Yes, we've met earlier."

"Okay, in college or school?" asked an impatient Laila.

"She's the girl my parents wanted me to marry. She is the same Shivani whom I had met. I hope you remember! You were after my life as you wanted me to move on."

Laila was speechless, partly due to an awkward recollection of a rough patch in their relationship and partly due to realizing that Ron's discomfort still persisted after all these years. A major part of their walk up to Laila's place was blanketed by silence, thereafter.

That night, Laila didn't sleep, even for a minute. She tried to, but thoughts about Ron kept coming back to her mind. She said to herself, "Had Ron married Shivani, he would have been in a different world. He would have had a beautiful wife who would deck up traditionally, and children like that cute girl. His family would have been complete. He could have lived with them comfortably, and moved about in his circle as a happily married man. His parents would have got the chance to pamper his kids." Her mind kept going back to the guilt that had earlier pushed her to convince him to move on. Once again, she cursed herself for Ron's fate.

The next day, she was not in a good mood so she postponed an important plan. Actually, Ron had enthusiastically convinced her to learn how to drive a scooter. According to Ron, the open area in the village was the best for her to learn to drive. When Ron arrived with his brother's scooter, she feigned illness. "Ron, I have a headache and I don't think it's a good idea to drive with a headache," Laila said.

Ron's excitement fizzled out but he was more concerned about Laila. "Stop working around the house, take some medicine, and rest," he advised.

She replied in an agitated manner, "Let me be on my own. I'll be fine. It's just that I can't take the driving lesson today. Don't waste your time over here. We shall meet later when I feel better."

A perplexed Ron retorted, "What's wrong with you? Why are you being so rude to me?"

Laila was emotionally so disturbed that she grabbed his hand and told him to go. Ron was surprised with her behaviour and he thought, "Perhaps she's angry that I didn't socialise with Shivani's husband or maybe someone from the neighbourhood would have made nasty comments about our friendship." He let her be and returned home to come back after an hour or so.

When she closed the door, Raashi's words suddenly echoed in her mind. Raashi had asked her once, "What is Ron's fault?" She knelt down crying inconsolably and later rang up Ron and said, "Ron, I'm sorry. Please come back.".

He rushed to her place and caressed her as he understood that she was going through emotional turmoil. She told Ron, "Shivani called me this morning. She thanked me for the courtesies extended to all of them. She also asked me not to waste a lifetime waiting for the right moment. She advised me to acknowledge the unseen and unheard level of attachment you have towards me. She strongly felt that both of us need to be together."

Ron didn't want Laila to think any further about the issue. "I never knew that my strong girl can be shaken by small emotional storms. We are good the way we are.

There is nothing more to it! Now, quickly freshen up, and get ready to learn driving. Mind you, I'm not taking no for an answer." He wiped her tears away and within an hour they were seen on the scooter, swerving on the road, with Laila finding it hard to balance. He gave her two hours of driving lessons after which she confidently drove the scooter on a deserted stretch all by herself.

"Finally, after many years of convincing from all quarters, I learned driving. All thanks to you. Mrs Samson will be very happy to hear the news," Laila said, with a broad smile on her face.

On reaching Delhi, Ron spent a couple of hours at Mrs Samson's house before boarding the train to his duty station. Ron, Laila and Mrs Samson chatted to their heart's content, as there was so much to discuss: The wedding functions, the gifts that Nina had received and the reunion with relatives. Mrs Samson loved such talk and so did Laila. Before Ron left, he proudly flaunted the watch that he had received from Laila as a gift.

The next day, Laila shared all the videos and photos with Mrs Samson. Laila pointed to Nina in a picture and said, "Madam, see her saree! It's the one that you had gifted her. She wore it for the prayer ceremony. All the ladies wanted to know where she had bought it from. She proudly told them that it was a gift from her loving DG. And what can I say about the beaded jewellery set that you gave to her? Everyone appreciated it a lot. Most ladies in the village don't get the opportunity to own such exquisite jewellery. They were fascinated."

Laila's phone rang. It was Nina. She wanted to talk to Mrs Samson. "Hello DG, how have you been? We missed you so much during the wedding," Nina said, pulling Ravi into the frame so that he could also greet her.

"Hello, Aunty. Hope you are doing well," said Ravi.

"Oh, my sweethearts, I am fine. Congratulations to both of you. May God shower his blessings on you. When are you coming to meet me?"

"Very soon DG. When we go on our honeymoon, we will stop over in Delhi. Our trip is booked for next week."

Sakhi also came forward and congratulated Nina.

Laila noticed something peculiar. She could sense that Nina had to force Ravi to talk to them. However, she thought that maybe he was tired. She ignored it and went to bed.

Dry and parched fields do hold some lifeless seeds.
Once water trickles down the cracks, many hearts bleed.

32

The Short-lived Calm

A week after Ron re-joined duty, he was informed about his upcoming posting. He told Laila that his unit was moving to a field area. This distressed Laila as field area postings for the families of defence personnel are synonymous with trying times and stress. However, she suppressed the manifestations of nervousness and wished him all the luck. He was to move in a couple of days.

A month into Nina's marriage, when the new couple didn't go on their honeymoon, Laila casually asked her, "What about your trip?"

"We had to cancel the trip because Ravi's father fell sick. He had an angioplasty. He's fine now."

"You didn't mention this to me. At least, I could have made a courtesy call to your mother-in-law. Be more careful about these kinds of familial formalities, Nina!"

Nina understood her concern and apologized.

Meanwhile, Laila got promoted as the area manager of the NGO. It was a major achievement for her and the perfect reciprocation from the management for her selfless, dedicated and innovative work. When she told Ron about it, his joy knew no bounds. Mrs Samson was also thrilled to hear the news.

A few days later, a surprise gift arrived for Laila. Ron had sent her an electric scooter. She was excited and nervous to receive it. Mrs Samson said, "Ron is such a gem. He has done the right thing. You must use this now. It will protect your knees from the damage caused by using rickshaws."

"This is the perfect gift for you," Raju said, as he parked it inside the compound. Mrs Samson insisted that it be kept inside.

Laila began driving the scooter around the colony soon although she did it under Raju's guidance initially. One day, she sent Ron a video of herself driving the scooter. She expected him to respond when he got back from work. Surprisingly, he didn't reply. She waited for his call till late into the night. She tried calling him, but his phone wasn't reachable.

She got anxious and obviously, she couldn't sleep. The next morning the situation remained the same. As he was posted in a forward area, she had an even more nerve-wracking experience. She was glued to the news channels throughout the day. Late at night, Ron called and told her that he and his team were in a sensitive counterinsurgency operation. Thankfully, none of them had sustained any severe injuries and the emergency operation had been successfully completed. Laila could barely speak as she almost choked on her tears, but she managed to say, "You nearly gave me a heart attack, but you always do us proud."

One evening, while returning home from the office, Laila bumped her scooter into a divider and suffered a fall. She injured her knee and was rushed to the emergency where the doctors found that in addition to her external injuries, two tiny pieces of cartilage had broken off and were stuck in her knee joint. She called Nina who then consulted an orthopaedic who advised her to get the tiny bits extracted as was advised by the doctor in Delhi. Laila underwent minor surgery. Ron wasn't able to be with her as he was on duty. Nina came over for a week to attend to Laila.

Mrs Samson's major needs were already being catered to by Sakhi, so everything seemed settled. Laila's wounds healed in a week's time. This time, when Nina visited, Laila noticed that she had changed drastically. Some changes were good: she became more organized and was more interested in cooking; she made an effort to dress up rather than lounge around the whole day in pyjamas! However, some changes bothered Laila. She noticed that Nina was dissatisfied and impatient about trivial things all the time. Her tone changed very often when she talked to Ravi on the phone. Laila assumed that it was due to the initial, sudden changes that married life had brought along.

A few days later, Laila got a call from Rita who sounded disturbed. "Mummy is down with typhoid. Brother and his family are on vacation," Rita said.

"Oh Lord, when did this happen? I talked to her just two days ago."

"She had fever and related symptoms. She might not have told you. The test came out positive yesterday," a disheartened Rita said.

"It must be so difficult for uncle to manage all alone."

"Yes, it is. I planned to leave the kids with their grandparents and visit the village for a week but they are also unwell."

Laila, in a sincere bid to help her out, said, "Don't worry. I can go there for a week if you are fine with it."

Soon, Laila was in the village taking care of Ron's ailing mother. It was a great relief for the elderly couple. The lady recovered and the day Laila was to leave for Delhi, a few neighbours dropped in. Laila overheard a conversation which disturbed her. One of the visitors told Ron's mother, "Don't praise Laila too much just because she attended to you for a few days. As long as she's friends with Ron, she'll be good to you. The day their friendship dissolves, she won't even take your call!" Although Laila remained calm, the denigration left her heartbroken.

Six months later, Nina visited her once again for a few days. One day, when she was rude to Ravi over the phone, Laila asked her, "What's the matter? Can't you talk decently to him?"

"This is my personal matter. I will handle it my way."

Laila reprimanded her and told her to respect her relationship with Ravi. Nina walked away to the lawn. Laila could make out that she was crying. When she didn't come back after a good ten minutes, Laila went to check on her. Nina hugged Laila and cried inconsolably. Laila's motherly instincts pointed towards possible trouble in Nina's paradise.

Ravi's behaviour had changed post-marriage, at least Nina thought so. She told Laila, "Whenever we have an extra day off, he always wants to visit his parents. I told him that I'd like to meet you and DG in Delhi. He just puts it off for later. I don't feel very welcome at my in-laws' place too."

Laila listened patiently and then she said, "But this is how marriage is. It is new for both of you. You might take some time to adjust. It'll work only if you respect each other and each other's wishes."

"But he never tries to…" Nina began.

Laila interrupted her. "Listen, Nina, his family is new to you and yours is new to him. Moreover, his father has been unwell lately. Both of you must find your place as a couple in your respective families. It is no more a matter of just you and him."

Nina began to get the hang of things. She realised that she was being excessively demanding. Laila had pacified her that day, but the seeds of doubt had been sown. She began to worry about the fate of Nina's marriage. She knew that Nina found it tough to adopt a moderate approach towards many things in life. She was more of a hothead. Amidst clouds of doubt, Laila found solace by focusing on the scant yet existent positives in life.

**Transitory are moments, both of tranquillity and turmoil.
Non-flowering plants also contribute to fertility of the soil.**

33

Laila—The Star

One evening when Laila was in the lawn, admiring the plump roses, her phone rang. It was a call from her village. Savita, her cousin, needed help. "My mother had a terrible fall and she's fractured her leg," said Savita.

"What! How did she fall?"

"While working on a railway track…she was repairing the track with other labourers when her foot got stuck in the track and she fell."

"Where is aunty now?"

"We took her to the medical facility nearby, but they said that the x-ray showed a completely broken bone and she'll need advanced surgery. Aunt Suguna suggested that I call you for advice."

"Okay. What is the current situation?"

"They've put a temporary cast but she's in terrible pain."

"Give me ten minutes. I'll talk to Nina and get back to you."

Nina arranged an ambulance to reach the remote area. Laila conveyed the information to Savita. When she was about to end the call, Savita hesitantly said, "Didi, we don't have enough money for the surgery. I need time to sell my gold chain to pay for it."

"Oh…I should have asked you about it! How much do you need?"

"I have two thousand rupees with me, and I've arranged another thousand through my friend. But the estimate is around twenty thousand."

"Umm…let me think of something." Suddenly, it struck her that Ron's brother could help. She called him and transferred money into his account. She requested him to give Savita the cash as soon as possible. Being a contractor, he often dealt in cash, so it was readily available to him.

In the evening, Laila called Savita to enquire about her mother's health. Savita told her that the doctors had to put a rod to hold the bone in place. However, the surgery was successful and she was under observation. Savita told Laila, "Didi, I don't have the words to thank you. You've helped in the time of need. I will return the money once I sell my chain."

In an authoritative tone, Laila said, "Don't you dare, Savita. Forget about the money. Is she only your mother? You don't have to return anything. Let me know if you need more money." Savita didn't have any words to express her gratitude.

A few days later, Laila's aunt was discharged from the hospital. When she reached home, Savita told her everything in detail. She called Laila immediately and thanked her for her benevolence. Laila felt relieved and told Savita to keep in touch.

Ron was turning forty-two. He was temporarily in Meerut, staying in the Officer's Mess. Meerut is an ancient city in Uttar Pradesh. It is a three-hour drive from Delhi. Laila had planned a grand surprise for him on his birthday. She had not shared her plans with anyone except Mrs

Samson, and that too, just a day before she left for Meerut. One of his closest friends, Major Girish and his wife, were also posted in Meerut. Laila had become friends with the lady as she had met her on an earlier trip and they got along well. They shared common interests and Laila often connected with her over the phone. The couple was gracious enough to let Laila plan the celebration at their residence. She reached there on the eve of his birthday. She just told him that she wanted to spend the day with him. He was on cloud nine to have her there. She arrived an hour late. Immediately, they headed for dinner at a restaurant in the vicinity.

When they came back, it was 11:30 p.m. They relaxed and had coffee. As soon as the clock struck twelve, the doorbell rang. Ron was surprised to see Rita and her husband at the door. They came in and the gala celebration began. Ron cut the cake and they chatted till 2:00 a.m.

In the morning, while Ron and Major Girish went to work, Laila and Rita shopped at the local market. High tea was planned for the evening. A few more couples had been invited. Laila and Rita were busy preparing a cake and snacks. Rita intermittently checked on her kids via video call. They were with their paternal grandparents for two days. It was Laila's idea to have Rita and her husband surprise Ron, and he was overjoyed.

When Ron cut the cake that evening, Laila offered him a bowl of chits and said, "Choose one." Assuming it was a kind of game, he playfully picked one. When he read it, tears of joy rolled down his cheeks. "What does it say, Brother?" Rita asked. Ron stared at Laila for a while, and then hugged her. It was a "Let's promise" note.

Rita was so happy that she gave Laila a tight hug and kissed her. She just couldn't stop thanking her. "You've given him the best gift ever," she said. She video-called her parents back in the village, and in their virtual presence, the rings were exchanged. Laila had brought along two gold bands.

It was a surreal moment for Ron, the best moment of his life! Laila also felt content and liberated. She had finally given herself and Ron the long-deserved chance.

The bird of fondness may take time to fly high,
But it does make it one day and in style.

34

Inquisitive Parents

Back in Delhi, Laila was concerned about Mrs Samson, as her health was deteriorating rapidly. Her partial paralysis had returned and she was bedridden once again. Eric visited with his wife Donna for a fortnight.

During her initial years at Mrs Samson's house, Laila had noticed that whenever Eric visited, some argument ensued between him and his mother which left Mrs Samson feeling hurt and troubled. It was only later that he realised that he needed to be more considerate given her advancing age.

This time around, it was his wife whose insensitive attitude towards the old lady brought bitterness back to their equation. Donna was indifferent to Mrs Samson's failing health and called her friends every other day for lunch, games and dinner during her visit. Often, she didn't even bother to greet Mrs Samson in the morning, let alone ask about her wellbeing. She would go shopping and then return home late in the evening with bag-loads of stuff. She habitually criticized Laila, and later Sakhi too for their style of cooking. She frequently ordered food from outside and when she fell sick she would blame the contaminated water, even though top-quality water purifiers had been installed in the house.

Although all the gatherings happened on the first floor, the octogenarian felt neglected. When she mentioned it to her son, he assured her that he'd talk to Donna. In reality, he was more of a hen-pecked husband, especially when his wife was around. Laila thought, "Eric's emotions fluctuate dramatically, his inclinations are never clear, they keep changing." But she gave him the benefit of doubt. She told Mrs Samson, "At least he tries to maintain a balance. He has to keep it harmonious both ways. And he never lets you remain upset!"

Time passed by but Mrs Samson's health didn't improve. However, she was stable. On a bright morning, she casually asked Laila, "So, when are you planning to get married?"

"No marriage on the cards, Madam. We've promised each other a lifetime of togetherness, and that is enough for both of us."

"What promise? No, no, now you can't shy away from marriage."

Laila wiped Mrs Samson's face after she had finished feeding her the porridge for breakfast. "Madam, you know us so well. We are happy this way. We are there for each other and we are together in our own special world. If and when we feel the need, we'll get married. But we aren't there yet," she said. She gave Mrs Samson her medicines and proceeded to get ready for work.

Laila had a crucial meeting that day with a top business head from the city who intended to donate a substantial amount of money to the NGO. She had been given the task of briefing him about the activities taken up to promote the welfare of underprivileged children.

In the evening when she reached home, she excitedly told Mrs Samson, "What a great day it has been! Mr David was impressed by the presentation that my colleagues and I had prepared. He even asked me about my background and my association with the NGO."

"Really? Did you tell him how you first started working at the age of eighteen?"

"Yes, and when we had a casual interaction afterwards, he said that my life's story is a perfect example of women's empowerment. He was so appreciative of the way you have supported me." As she spoke, she realised that Mrs Samson had fallen asleep. She covered her with a quilt, tucked it properly, switched off the lights and went to her room.

A few days later, when Laila spoke to Ron's mother, she had to explain herself again when she mentioned that they were eager to see Laila and Ron as a married couple. Seeing the kind of life and societal norms that the older generation had experienced, it was difficult for Laila and Ron to explain their outlook to the elders. Both tried their best to clearly and respectfully convey their thoughts.

For the initial six months, it was hard for Ron's parents to digest that they wouldn't get married even though, according to them, the engagement had taken place. When they were told that with the exchange of rings, Laila and Ron had promised each other a lifetime of unconditional togetherness, they were left with no choice but to make peace with the situation.

Ron's mother needed some more convincing which Laila happily did but his father told Laila, "We are happy if both of you are happy. Times have changed now, and both partners in a relationship are equal. As long as you complete and complement each other, there's no need for anything else. Our blessings are always with you."

The demand for clarifications can surely create unease. However, explaining your position is better than choosing to appease.

35

Nina Moves Abroad

Back at Nina's place, the couple was elated to have bagged work contracts abroad. An excited Nina called Laila to inform her about the same. After a long time, she sounded happy and excited. "They need to grab this opportunity to improve their economic prospects as well as their relationship," Laila thought. "Nina, listen carefully. You've got this opportunity, and I'm very happy for you. You must work on both your job and marriage. This opportunity that you've been blessed with will never come back. There will be the struggles of settling in a new country, among new people, but don't let anything affect your marriage. Discover for yourself the balance that will strengthen your relationship. I'm sure you'll be much happier," she advised Nina who paid attention to what Laila had to say and promised to work on it.

Ravi's parents were ecstatic to hear about the development. They had eyed the prospects of their son settling abroad, and their own immigration at a later time, although they didn't mention it to him. Even if they had, it wouldn't have made a difference, as he was oblivious of the fact that this was a major factor that could change the course of his married life.

For Nina, it was a honeymoon trip that was planned with just a one-way ticket. She was happy and positive about going abroad. She had been living alone since her college days, so there was no question of being homesick. Laila though was worried as she was going to miss her little sister a lot.

Bags were packed and both left Hyderabad for Delhi. In Delhi, they stopped over at Mrs Samson's house for one day. Basically, they reached late in the evening and were to catch their flight the next evening. Mrs Samson was seeing them for the first time after their wedding. She told Laila to arrange for a cake and flowers so that they could have a small celebration.

The couple spent the next day visiting the local market and a temple to pray and get blessings for their new journey. After having a light meal, they took a nap and jetted off in the evening. Raju went to drop them at the airport. Laila couldn't go because Sakhi had taken the day off and Mrs Samson couldn't be left all alone. Nina was happy and excited, but Laila had tears in her eyes when they said their goodbyes.

Later, Laila revealed her emotions to Mrs Samson saying, "Empty nest syndrome! Today, I understood the feeling that you've been experiencing for years! It is so tough to let your children go miles and miles away. But it is their life, so they get to decide, I guess."

A couple of months passed by, and Laila often found herself at the receiving end of Nina's frustrations and tears. It is undoubtedly difficult for any professional or student to leave one's homeland and settle in a new country with vast cultural differences. Nina's experience was no different. Laila patiently counselled her every time to make things easier for her. Within a few months, Nina got the hang of things and the challenges started to vanish.

She made new friends, understood the work culture, adjusted to the routines, got a driver's licence, and finally her equation with Ravi returned to normal as it was before their wedding. One day, Laila said to Mrs Samson, "Madam, perhaps the sudden responsibilities and formalities that come with marriage had overwhelmed Nina, disrupting her married life."

"Yes, even I believe that once the two of them figure things out for themselves, they'll be in a better position to attend to their family, be it the emotional or financial needs."

Ron was due for a promotion and so his mother and brother went to meet him. It was a moment of great satisfaction and joy for them, as Ron had steadily climbed the ladder of success and was to become a Lieutenant Colonel. Mrs Samson gifted a customised silver bracelet to Ron when he visited. She had a special liking for him.

Back in the foreign land, Nina and Ravi started travelling to nearby towns for weekend getaways and she sent pictures and videos to Laila from scenic locations. On the work front, she was impressed with the protocols in the hospital. She told Laila, "Everything is so perfect and streamlined. The level of hygiene at the hospital is beyond imagination. There is no shortage of staff and we have comfortable rooms to rest during break time. Paging systems are in place and the doctors at the hospital are so committed to their duty."

"It's good to know that you like it there. Don't forget all that I've told you earlier."

Nina went to great lengths to reassure her.

Eight months down the line, Ravi's mother said to him, "Ravi, your father's health is fine now. I think it will be a good change if you arrange for our trip. We can come and stay with you for a month or so. We miss you a lot." Ravi agreed and Nina also supported him. She was now in a better frame of mind to adjust to changes.

When Laila came to know about it, she anticipated minor issues. But she didn't let any of her thoughts reach Nina. She said, "It's good to hear this. You will have company. It will be a good chance to build a cosier connection with your in-laws. Try to know their likes and dislikes and be very respectful."

Nina giggled saying, "As if I'm going to fight! Of course, I'll try my best and I'm sure we'll have a great time."

Parent-child relationship is surely a complex one;
While a parent, mostly, has to hold back emotions,
The child is the one who has all the options.

Trouble in Paradise

Instructed strictly by his mother to arrive on time at the airport, Ravi stood there staring endlessly at the flight information display screen. As a result of the delayed flight, he gorged on coffee and sandwiches from his favourite fast-food chain, unbothered about the resultant bloating.

To celebrate the arrival of her in-laws, Nina had decorated the main entrance with jasmine flowers. Embroidered curtains and sofa-backs enhanced the ambience of the hall. Fresh roses in the vases across all corners perfumed the air. It was a one-bedroom-hall-kitchen unit. They vacated the bedroom for the parents and decided to manage with the sofa-cum-bed in the living room. She had prepared a traditional Indian sweet dish to welcome them.

As soon as the car entered the driveway, Nina, who was dressed in beautiful traditional attire, rushed towards the door. Ravi guided his parents towards the main entrance. She touched their feet and welcomed them. Meanwhile, Ravi wheeled in their huge bags – the first shock!

"Where will these bags rest?" Nina thought. She immediately ignored the thought and made the parents comfortable in the living room. Ravi's mother remarked, "You have a TV like ours, I thought you'd have a large screen TV." Nina smiled and went to the kitchen to fetch water and juice for them.

After parking the car in the garage, a visibly tired Ravi entered and carelessly dumped three overcoats on a corner table. "Oh, no!" he exclaimed, as he slumped on the couch. A smashing noise was heard. Nina came running from the kitchen, only to see a broken vase and strewn flowers. Without showing disappointment, she moved the coats to another table. Then, she cleaned up the mess. The parents were jetlagged, so they went off to sleep after having their meal.

Days passed by and many such incidents pricked Nina. Sometimes, her mother-in-law would complain that she woke up late. At other times, she didn't like the taste of her tea. Nina patiently handled everything. She poured her heart out to Laila on her way to work. Laila was her agony aunt during this tough time!

One day, they all went to a mall and while she was having a look at a handbag for her mother-in-law, Nina met one of her friends. She introduced her to the parents-in-law. When they returned home, Nina's mother-in-law said to her, "Your friend looked so beautiful. Why don't you groom yourself like her?"

Nina retorted, "Mom, she's a model. Looking good is a part of her profession. I'm a nurse, and my job demands that my nails are cut and my hair is tied up neatly."

A few days later, Nina's mother-in-law gave her a long list of cosmetics sent by her sister-in-law, Chhavi. They were really expensive items, so Nina showed the list to Ravi. To her dismay, a disinterested Ravi said, "Handle it yourself. It's a matter between you ladies. Keep me out of it!"

Nina had taken a week off from work so that she could show her in-laws around. When Nina's leave came to an end, things got tough for her, as she had to cook food for her in-laws every evening after returning home from the hospital. Her mother-in-law had categorically told her on arrival, "Your father can't digest reheated, frozen food. Cook fresh food for him and a portion for me too." Somehow, Nina managed, telling herself that it was just a matter of one month.

One day, she overheard her mother-in-law's conversation with Chhavi. "Why don't you also come over for two weeks while we are here? Ravi can complete the formalities for your visa. You can enjoy with us and all three of us can fly back together." Nina got the shock of her life. She couldn't even think of adjusting to the presence of another member in the house and that too Chhavi, with all her tantrums!

Overwhelmed by frustration, she discussed the matter with Ravi who told her, "Don't worry, if Chhavi comes, we'll rent another apartment for a month." Nina just stared at him, appalled. She thought, "We're earning a limited amount of money barely enough for ourselves. A host of added expenses will set us back financially by six months if not more." She was not averse to Chhavi's visit, but she didn't want it to happen just then.

Ravi wasn't able to get her point and an argument ensued. Over the next few days, she lost her zeal and patience. Minor disagreements started turning into arguments which then took the shape of ugly quarrels.

One day, she put her foot down, and quit her job without informing Ravi. She booked a flight ticket home and informed Ravi just before leaving. When Nina reached India, she called Laila and apprised her of the situation. Laila was shaken up.

Laila called Ravi for an explanation. He seemed indifferent and left her speechless saying, "Nina was disrespectful to my parents, and I couldn't tolerate it. So, I didn't stop her from leaving. She should apologise first and only then can she come back." His shameless and ruthless behaviour was unanticipated.

Meanwhile, Harsh had turned into a dedicated and sincere doctor. He was just one year into his job as a junior doctor when destiny snatched his mother from him. Sarita had been under treatment for several years. She endured immense suffering and later when she developed a serious intestinal issue, she passed away. This loss shook him to the core. Disturbed by his mother's suffering, he often discussed her condition with senior doctors at the hospital where he worked. According to them, the condition wasn't life-threatening; however, an unfortunate and acute reaction to some medicines aggravated her condition and her body couldn't tolerate it.

Harsh came to terms with the reality that, sometimes, even medical science fails to answer questions put forth by destiny. Times were tough, and Laila tried her best to stay in touch with the disheartened young boy. "I have long known the pain caused by the loss of a parent. I must try to cheer him up. He needs to overcome the sadness," she thought.

Mrs Samson told Raju, "Try spending maximum time with Harsh when he's off-duty." They were all one big family. With time's healing touch, the pain was replaced by fond memories of Sarita.

Harsh's loss turned him into an even more compassionate and empathetic doctor. Gradually, he started to climb the ladder of success. Simultaneously, he started to prepare for an entrance examination to a post-graduate course. He had a cherished dream of becoming a neurosurgeon. Raju would bring Harsh along, occasionally, to meet and get blessings from Mrs Samson. After all, she had supported his entire education and Harsh also felt indebted to her.

On one such visit, an inquisitive Harsh asked Mrs Samson about her medicines. Little did he know about Pandora's box that he had opened. "Oh, my child, my very own doctor, I'm glad you've asked me this question. Come, sit here," said Mrs Samson, as she extended her hand towards Harsh. He got up from his seat, held her hand and sat beside her excitedly. Meanwhile, she told Laila, "Get my box of medicines, and tell him all about them. After all, you only take care of my medication schedule."

Laila smiled and for a fraction of a second, looked towards Raju, disapproving the timing of Harsh's question. Both knew that it would be a long discussion.

Anyhow, Laila got the box and then Mrs Samson started off, "I take six tablets right after breakfast and three at night. So, tell me what is this green one for?"

Harsh had a look at the blister pack and said, "This one controls your blood pressure, Aunty."

"Oh, I see. It tastes so bitter."

"And what about these two capsules? I take these too."

"One takes care of your acidity problem and the other is a multivitamin."

"This multivitamin has a horrible smell though."

"I second that, Aunty."

Laila told Mrs Samson, "Madam, let him take a look at the medicines. Meanwhile, I'll check if lunch is ready. Sakhi is preparing a delicious spread today!"

"No, no. She will manage. You stay here so that you also get to know about the medicines," Mrs Samson said.

To top it all, an overexcited Harsh started elaborating on the possible side effects and food interactions. Laila signalled Raju to stop Harsh from prolonging the conversation further. The old lady had already been guided by the doctors about what to take and when. However, due to her advanced age, she couldn't retain all of it. Still, she endlessly double-checked whenever Laila gave her the medicines. Both Laila and Raju were aware of the unsatiable quest that Mrs Samson had developed regarding her medicines. After all, they had been accompanying her to her doctor's appointments for ages.

When the situation was about to get out of hand, Laila brought the food to the table. To everyone's surprise, Mrs Samson said, "First, Harsh will check my blood pressure, and then we'll eat."

"No! No blood pressure now, we must eat the food while it's hot. Madam, the BP monitor is automatic, so it won't make a difference if I do it or Harsh does it," Laila said firmly. She literally grabbed Harsh's hand and took him towards the table and all of them had lunch.

A year down the line, despite Laila's best efforts, Nina and Ravi got divorced. By then, Nina was once again settled in her job at Hyderabad, but she was yet to address the emotional hurt that pricked her all the time.

Often, Laila called her over to Delhi on the weekends. Sometimes, she would go to Hyderabad herself. She had the task of reviving Nina's cheerfulness. Once, Laila took Nina along with her to meet Ron too. She assured Nina that she had her back and gradually, over the next six months, Nina returned to normalcy.

Architectural complexity of the brain
Lends tortuosity to the mind.
Many out there know the art
Of not letting their true side unwind,
Leaving us with the only option
Of growing cautious with time.

37

On Pins and Needles

Ron was constantly fatigued by the ongoing chronic complaints of gastrointestinal issues and electrolyte imbalance. His long-standing liver ailment was turning refractory, and his condition had deteriorated over the last few months. The doctor advised a liver transplant. Laila roped in Nina to consult specialists in the field and shared Ron's reports with her. Unfortunately, all the opinions turned out to be the same. Laila and Rita went to Bangalore, where he was posted. Rita left her kids with her husband as the situation at Ron's place was tense.

It was going to be a major surgery, and the doctors had informed them that the survival rate was low due to his existing condition. But surgery was the only option to save his life. Tremendous courage was required from each of them to take this decision. Since saving his life was the ultimate aim, they had to take the chance.

Laila woke up early each day to visit a temple in the vicinity. Offering flowers and fruits at the temple, she prayed for Ron's wellbeing. Out of nervousness, Rita often cried, burying her head in Laila's arms. Laila comforted her every time. Thankfully, a donor was available, and since the profile matched, the surgery was planned.

The day Ron was to be admitted to the hospital, Laila took him along with her to the temple. Her face radiated a different glow. Perhaps she was confident that Ron was going to be okay or perhaps she just wanted him to feel confident. But surely, there was no sign of jitteriness. She sat beside him, retrieved a gold ornament from her clutch, and gently placed it in his hand. Ron asked, "What is this?" A glance at the ornament left him speechless. It was a Mangal sutra, a sacred piece that signifies marriage. "No Laila, I can't do this to you. What if I don't survive this surgery? I don't want to bind you in a relationship just to leave you alone. I can't do this," Ron objected.

A teary-eyed Laila replied, "Just don't talk like this. You'll be fine. I know it." A low-key ceremony followed and the priest solemnised their marriage. When it was time to tie the Mangal sutra, his hands started shaking from the scary unpredictability of life. She helped him tie the Mangal sutra around her neck. As surreal as it was, they walked out of the temple as a married couple!

When they reached home, Rita opened the door and couldn't stop staring in disbelief. It was totally unexpected. She hugged both of them and cried like a child. They informed the family in Dehradun over a video call. The news couldn't wash off the anxiety over the surgery, but it was calming like a breeze for his parents.

An hour later, they went to the hospital. Once Ron got admitted, all the preliminary investigations were done. Rita was anxious and disturbed. Ron told her, "Don't be so sad, little sister! You'll make me cry." He succeeded in bringing a smile to her face.

Laila said, "Rita, your brother is a gem. Only good things will come his way. He'll be fine. You must be optimistic and strong. Just pray to The Almighty for his recovery." She hugged Rita to reassure her although she herself felt uncertain and anxious.

Sounding unconvincing wasn't an option for Laila. She reiterated to Ron, "Tomorrow, after the surgery, you'll get permanent relief from this ailment. You'll feel much better."

"I hope I don't get permanent relief from everything else too."

His tone was humorous but his words were enough to evoke her deepest fears in the form of tears. He held her hand tightly and said, "If you cry, who will give me the strength?"

"I'm not crying, and you don't need strength from me. You are my superhero!" she exclaimed, trying to pacify him.

When it was time for the surgery, Laila told Ron, "Go and fight it out. From now till forever, I promise to sincerely share with you the responsibility of Mummy, Papa and the entire Sharma family, our family." With a smile on her face and confidence in her eyes, she wished him the best for the surgery. As they held hands, for the first time ever, both felt a new stream of energy flowing through. As he was wheeled into the pre-operative room, Laila blew him a kiss and he smiled in contentment.

The surgery was going to take about eight hours. Throughout, Laila kept praying for Ron's wellbeing. Rita was by her side, keeping her parents updated about the developments. When the surgery was over, they were told that the doctors had done their bit and they had to wait and see how Ron's body reacted to the procedure in the next seventy-two hours. The situation continued to remain tense. Both Rita and Laila expected to hear a more comforting update.

About twelve hours later, he regained consciousness, and everyone thought that although late, the positive news had started to trickle in. Within two hours, his body started showing strange reactions and a pall of gloom started to descend. The girls informed Ron's brother about each and every development in detail, but the update was filtered before it reached his parents, as they were old and wouldn't be able to take the stress. The doctors tried their best but just when things seemed to be going out of hand, he was airlifted to Delhi and taken to a premier medical facility of the defence forces.

Ron's brother repeatedly insisted that he wanted to be with them in Bangalore, but Rita and Laila convinced him to stay back with the parents. When Ron was shifted, his brother didn't wait and flew to Delhi.

Both Laila and Rita were distressed. He tried to comfort them. Ron was taken in promptly and his treatment was initiated in the ICU. Ron's brother urged the women to rest while he was there. At home, Laila and Rita didn't reveal much of the details to the old lady, but the vermillion on her hair and the Mangal sutra attracted her attention. Laila then told her about her impromptu decision. Mrs Samson kissed her on the forehead. It was a tough time. There was no scope for even a single smile, just deep concern!

Putting others before oneself,
Sincere commitment suffices in itself.

38

Recovery and Then a Huge Loss

Miracles do happen and that's what happened in Ron's case too. Backed by prayers and good wishes, he showed signs of improvement within the first week of treatment. Thereafter, he continued on the road to recovery. Subsequently, he re-joined duty. Laila accompanied him for a week so that he could get adequate rest. She managed the housework for him. They got their marriage registered.

Later, Laila and Ron visited their village together. Nina joined them there for a week. There was a gala celebration at Ron's place. Laila was officially welcomed to the family. All the post-wedding ceremonies were completed tastefully at Ron's place. Laila's aunts jointly hosted a celebratory lunch for Ron and his family. Gifts and sweets were exchanged. Ron's brother also hosted a formal reception for the couple where family members from both sides were invited. Friends and neighbours were invited too. All in all, it was a beautiful time they had in the village.

Afterwards, Laila, Ron and Nina headed back to Delhi. Nina spent another three days with Laila and her lovely DG, who was now frailer than ever.

Mrs Samson insisted that Laila stay with Ron for a few days every month. However, she visited only a couple of times as Mrs Samson's health was very delicate, and she didn't want the old lady to feel neglected. Ron understood this and was completely fine with it. After another six months, Mrs Samson was completely bedridden. Oftentimes, she had to be given parenteral nutrition. When Roger and Irene came to visit her that year, they were extremely disturbed. Irene even extended her stay by a couple of weeks to spend more time with Mrs Samson. Everyone around Mrs Samson tried to make her feel comfortable with their small efforts. Just before leaving, Irene had a premonition that the situation would go from bad to worse. It was difficult but they had to go.

One day, after Mrs Samson was fed lunch by Laila, she slept not to wake up again. She passed away peacefully in her sleep. When Laila brought her evening tea and tried to wake her up, she realised that her body was cold. She immediately felt a deep void inside. A doctor was called. He broke the sad news to Laila, Sakhi and Raju, as they stood around Mrs Samson's bed. This time around, Laila had lost her Godmother. She informed Irene and Mrs Samson's close friends immediately.

After a couple of days, in the presence of all her near and dear ones, Mrs Samson's last rites were performed. Ron stood there thinking, "She earned so much goodwill in her lifetime. Everyone who's here to bid her goodbye has tears in their eyes and praise for her on their lips." The old lady left an indelible mark with her benevolence, grace, cheerful nature and love for humanity.

A week later, as Laila and Sakhi were preparing breakfast, Irene entered the kitchen asking for some water. Laila gave it to her, and she signalled Laila to come into a room where they could talk privately. Laila followed and Irene asked her, "Do you know about mom's will?"

"No, but I guess it should be with the family lawyer. I'll give you his contact number."

"No, no. I mean to say, do you know what mom-in-law has passed on to you?"

"Passed on to me? No, I have no idea. Actually, why would she leave anything to me?"

A gleaming Irene informed a puzzled Laila that Mrs Samson had distributed her assets into three equal parts, two for her sons and one for Laila! She had left lump sums for Raju and Sakhi too. Laila started sweating profusely and couldn't react. Irene said, "I feel so blessed and proud to be the daughter-in-law of such a great personality. She has done justice to everyone."

Laila was reluctant to accept the idea, let alone the legacy! Irene cautioned her saying, "Donna is not in favour of this distribution and will try her best to oppose it. We all know that Eric won't have much say in this matter."

"But…why me?"

"No, Laila, promise me, you will honour the actual will. Don't refuse your share. If you relinquish it under pressure, Mom will be angry up there!"

All this was a little too much for Laila. She couldn't respond to Irene's call verbally, but just hugged her tightly and cried her heart out. Discussions and persuasions did happen, but because it was a legally registered will and the witnesses were there, Donna couldn't have her way.

Ron had returned to his duty immediately after the funeral, so he was not a part of the discussion. When he came to know about it, he was equally shocked. However, he managed to remark, "This shows how attached Mrs Samson was to you. Your dedication and commitment were unsurpassed. And Mrs Samson will live on in everyone's hearts."

The indelibility of kindness ensures that virtues spread;
Uniting compassionate souls, it is an invisible thread.

39

Back to the Roots

Years later, a two-story building stood at the site where Laila's home used to be. The signboard read, 'Atharva Care'. It was a branch office of the NGO that Laila used to work for when in Delhi. Young children were seen moving in and out of the building. Savita, Laila's cousin, was seen supervising the kids as they moved in and out of the facility in batches.

Some distance away, at Ron's place, three boys were playing basketball inside the gated area when Rita came from inside holding a tray with three glasses of milk. "Boys, take a break, it's milk time," she said. Her sons came to her while the third child ran towards his grandmother and said, "Granny, no milk. Give me chocolate, please." Little Atharva lovingly climbed onto her lap. "Yes, my darling," she replied, as she reached for the stash kept on the table near her cot.

A couple entered through the gate. Rita said to the little child, "See, Mom and Dad are back from work." As soon as Atharva saw them, he ran towards them, and Ron embraced him.

Laila, who stood by Ron's side, asked Atharva, "Son, you are eating chocolate again? How many have you had today?"

Ron's father, who had just returned from his yoga session said, "No, don't ask him that. It is his sixth birthday today, so he's allowed to have chocolate. Right, Atharva?"

"Yes," said the child smiling, as he gave the old man a high-five. Later, there was a cosy birthday celebration for Atharva.

Laila and Ron had adopted Atharva four years into their marriage. Ron took premature retirement and they settled in the village. The legacy that Mrs Samson had left behind for Laila was rightly used to establish 'Atharva Care' in the village. However, she did not accept a share in the immovable property. She relinquished it in favour of Roger and Irene. A new branch of the NGO was in the pipeline in another remote area of Dehradun, and Ron was spearheading it. Laila supervised the village branch. They helped their fellowmen get trained as educators, absorbing them into the cause.

Ron's brother was a successful contractor by this time and had shifted to the city with his family temporarily. Two years after her divorce, Nina remarried and later emigrated with her entrepreneur husband to America where she was blessed with a daughter whom they named Lina, a mix of Laila and Nina. It was Nina's way of showing gratitude and love to her elder sister.

By then, Laila and Ron had become a much-revered couple due to their social work. One day, when they were being felicitated at a function in Chakrata, Ron proudly said, "All credit goes to my wife, Laila. She has lived an exemplary life and continues to do so each day taking small yet effective steps despite the roadblocks. Throughout her life, she has selflessly worked for the people around her.

I have just supported her in her endeavours. She is the force behind this initiative and also 'Atharva Care.'" He then gave her the mic.

Laila thanked Ron and all the attendees. "When Atharva came into our lives and we relocated to the village, we felt the need to do something for the kids here. Decades ago, I had gone to Delhi searching for work and ended up finding a mother in Mrs Simi Samson. She made me who I am today." Laila couldn't speak any further. She looked towards the sky and blew a kiss. Loud applause echoed as the audience hailed the philanthropic couple. Little Atharva, sitting with his grandparents in the audience, was a sight to behold as he vigorously clapped with his tiny hands.

You can't say where you'll land
On an uncharted journey, when embarking;
Just let your best version emerge
And the result will be outstanding.